TEDDY

BY JOHN GAULT

BASED ON AN ORIGINAL SCREENPLAY BY IAN A. STUART

NOW AN UTTERLY HORRIFYING FILM

Encyclopocalypse Publications
www.encyclopocalypse.com

TEDDY

TEDDY

CHAPTER ONE

MAYBE, the boy thought, *I should warn the old guy; I should tell him about the hole.*

But instead he just watched, mildly fascinated, as the skinny old man picked his way between the grassy hummocks of the clearing, then stopped and raised a pair of binoculars to his eyes, making a clacking sound against his thick glasses. The old man turned slowly, sort of revolving on his feet, and swept the wall of trees that made the whole clearing into a natural room, open only to the sky. Then the old man stopped turning, bent his buzzard's neck forward, as if to get a better look, and fumbled a pad and pencil out of the flap pocket of his tweed jacket. He touched the pencil to the tip of his tongue—an odd gesture, the boy thought, one he'd never seen before—and laboriously wrote on the open page.

The boy, Jamie, had been in a reverie when he first sensed the intruder—for that, indeed, was what the old man was to him, the first person who'd ever come to this place, *his* place —but now he was fully returned to the present. Jamie leaned out, as far as was safely possible from his tree-branch perch twenty-five feet above the ground, and saw what had so interested the old man: a bird, a cedar waxwing, if Jamie wasn't mistaken. He returned his attention to the man. Seeing a waxwing was no big thing to Jamie, but this was his first birdwatcher. *If he stays where he is,* Jamie thought, *he'll be okay.*

And he wasn't moving, at least his feet weren't. In the weary, deliberate way that old people have, the man, whom Jamie now recognized as Reverend Marley or Morley or something like that, placed pencil and pad back in his pocket, lifted the binoculars to his eyes again—the clack sound repeated—and resumed his examination of the wall of trees. Instinctively, Jamie tried to hide, pressing himself close to the trunk of the great oak that had been his private domain ever since the spring. He did not want to be seen; he didn't need any more trouble, and he didn't want to answer any questions. Old Marley—or Morley—would demand to know what he was doing up there. Don't you know children aren't supposed to be playing in these woods, he would ask. What's your name? Where do you live? And then, Jamie guessed, Old Marley'd go back to town and tell Tom and Barbara about Jamie playing where he shouldn't be playing and they'd have to pretend they cared and punish him. He might not be able to come back here any more, to this "place."

It'd be just like what had happened when that frigging Miss Oliphant had told on him, had called up Barbara and yelled on the phone so loud that Jamie had heard her in the next room. He had tried to explain that it was an accident, that he hadn't meant to run into her wheelchair with his bicycle, but Barbara had said, "That didn't excuse the terrible things he said to the poor blind old woman."

"What things?" Jamie had asked, honestly not remembering.

"Now don't start that, Jamie," Barbara had said. "You know perfectly well!"

He peeked around the trunk to see if old Marley—no, it

was Morley, for sure—was still there. He was. Binoculars hanging against his chest, he was picking at something on his jacket; Jamie guessed it was burrs. Then Morley took up his stroll again, moving closer and closer to the hole but still not seeing it, his eyes searching everywhere but the ground. Jamie had to be impressed by how confidently the old man weaved between the mounds without looking down. He had a funny-looking cane. He probed in front of himself with it the way a blind man does, and it seemed to be giving messages directly to his feet.

Abruptly, the old man sat down on one of the lower hummocks, less than a dozen steps from the largest one, the one with the half-hidden hole, and began picking impatiently again at the burrs on his gray flannel pants. He was now no more than one hundred and fifty feet from Jamie's elevated vantage point, and the boy could even hear him humming something that he didn't recognize but guessed was some kind of hymn.

I wish Teddy was here, Jamie thought, suddenly. Teddy would know what to do. Whenever he felt confused about something, Teddy always seemed to have an answer.

He was still thinking about Teddy when the Reverend Morley rose and began walking again, pausing every couple of steps and cocking his head comically, so much like the birds he was so obviously fond of watching. Then his eyes went to the trunk of Jamie's oak and it followed it skyward. Jamie, caught off-guard, tried to move too quickly-not quickly enough to get safely behind the trunk, but too quickly for Morley to

miss him. He had given himself away.

"Say there, young man!"

Jamie crouched and pressed harder against the trunk, but he knew it was useless.

"I see you, young man!" The voice was rich and strong, which didn't seem right coming out of that turkey neck.

"Now come down here this instant! You have no business being in these woods! Can't you read signs?"

I wonder if he knows who I am, Jamie thought. There is still a chance he could slide down the rope and run off into the trees. He weighed that possibility for a second or two and decided that even if that did happen to work it wasn't the injuries—burned hands especially—that he might suffer. While part of his brain calculated his escape chances, another part gauged the old man's stride. He was not avoiding the mounds now, he was walking over the tops of them, his eyes never leaving Jamie, the funny-looking cane waving menacingly. Now he was standing on the biggest one, on the edge of the hole but obviously not aware of it, his mouth twitching and the sun flashing angrily off his glasses.

"Stop!" Jamie shouted. "Don't move."

"Don't you 'don't move' me, you pup," Old Morley sputtered. He may have been retired but he was still a man of God, and he was accustomed to respect. He wasn't going to take any lip from this brat or any other.

"No," Jamie pleaded, "Stop!"

The Reverend Morley stepped forward defiantly, and Jamie couldn't do any more for him. His mouth was open to shout again, and although no words came, it stayed that way in shocked disbelief. Everything seemed to happen so slowly after that. Even the old man's scream became an extended growl, like what happens on a tape recorder when the batteries are nearly dead. The earth under Morley's feet was falling away, but it was almost floating downward, as it gravity had lost its command of things, Jamie watched, transfixed, as each clump broke apart, hung in the empty air for long, long moments, then drifted down into the blackness of the hole.

Morley's feet must have hit something solid because suddenly—or as suddenly as things can stop in slow motion —his slide was ended. Jamie watched the anger that had been on the old man's face turn to shock, the mouth opening wide, the now-visible eyes—the glasses were hanging on some kind of chain or string on his man pitched forward, still in slow motion, into the hole, shock became fear, terrible distorting fear, and the old face down. There were no further screams.

Jamie stayed where he was, trying to focus on the black pit that had just sucked a human being into itself, and tried to listen for sounds of life from down there, sounds of activity. But his eyes burned and his ears rang and wild waves seemed to pound at his brain. Then, as suddenly as if nothing had ever happened, the world returned to normal.

He climbed carefully down the knotted rope, dropped the last few feet to the soft earth below, and walked out into the clearing, past the scrub brush toward the edge of the hole. He listened, but all he could hear were the normal forest sounds, the summer-buzz of high-tension lines just to the east, and the impatient growling of a semi changing gears out there on the highway. There were no sounds from the hole at all, no cry, no whimper, no breath.

Because he knew the hole very well, Jamie did not hesitate to walk almost all the way up to the lip. On one edge, the safe one, a dead tree was buried on its side, just below ground level, its roots holding back the soft-earth wall. But standing, Jamie could see nothing. The pit was at least twenty feet deep, maybe deeper, and the black soil seemed to drain and extinguish any light that touched it. Jamie dropped to his knees and then flat, his head and shoulders over the edge, his hands one over the other, flat, under his upper chest.

He waited as his eyes adjusted themselves to the near-darkness, and then his heart jumped and his breath left him. He had never seen death before, never experienced the ugliness of it. Sightless eyes fixed on him with hate and fear locked in them for all eternity. Jamie scrambled back, pushing away from the hole with his hands, propelling himself. For a moment he thought he was going to throw up, but the feeling passed.

Jamie knew he had to look again, that he had to be sure. After all, Barbara and Tom said he imagined things. He studied his hands, and they were real enough; the natural hum of the forest was the same as it always had been, as were the cars on the highway and the singing of the wires. And that, over there, the old man's cane, that's real. Jamie walked around the hole and picked it up where it had flown after Morley had fallen. He saw that it wasn't just a cane, but that it had a folding kind of top made of leather. Folded out, the top looked like a seat, a small seat. *I've never seen anything like this before*, Jamie thought, *so I can't be making it up: it must be real*. Carrying the "cane" the way Morley had, by the refolded handles, Jamie returned to his safe position and peered down once again, prepared this time for the twisted face of sudden death below.

But it wasn't there. Jamie blinked, and his mind raced. Then he smiled, because he understood. His friends had come out to see what was going on. Sure, he could hear them now, grunting away at one another, and sounding more excited than usual.

"Hey," he shouted, "it's me, Jamie. What's going on down there?"

The chattering stopped instantly, and another sound wafted up, the rustling, scraping sound of something heavy being dragged over soft earth, and Jamie's mind flashed to images of ants, out in his backyard, hauling ladybug corpses. Then, abruptly, there was silence from below. A few seconds later, the dragging noises resumed, but fading farther and farther away.

Jamie continued to lie there, concentrating on the dim patch of light that had, only a minute or so before, illuminated the dead face of the Reverend Morley. Maybe, he thought, they wouldn't let him see them today. Maybe they were upset about the man falling into their home. Which was how Jamie had come to regard that particular hole—as a home for his admittedly strange friends, a home that he visited regularly, every day, when he could. He hoped they didn't blame him for what had happened; it certainly hadn't been his fault, not this time.

"Is everything okay?" he asked, pretty sure that some of them were still around down there.

He didn't really expect an answer, but sometimes they'd jabber and grunt back at him, so he gave it a try anyway.

"Okay," he said finally, pushing himself to his feet. "It's okay. I'll come back tomorrow." He considered the cane for a moment, then tossed it down into the darkness. He saw a small gray hand reach into the circle of half-light and push at the stick with long, broken nails. Then the cane was snatched back into the gloom, and a pair of familiar yellow eyes blinked twice.

"I'm sorry for what happened," he said, his face serious again. "I tried to stop him, I really did!"

The eyes blinked twice more, then disappeared. Jamie broke into an easy jog until he reached the trees; then he stopped and looked back toward the hole, satisfied that it was still invisible to any casual observer, and slipped into the woods.

CHAPTER TWO

IF TOM and Barbara had asked him how he felt about leaving Jericho, Wisconsin, he probably would have said, sure, that was okay with him. That would have been true too a few months before. But now that he had his friends in the woods to visit and talk to every day, Jamie Benjamin thought that maybe he'd like to stay in this town. It didn't matter, though, because he didn't have a vote. After supper, when he'd tried to leave the table, Barbara had asked him to stay; she had some news for him. They were moving to Seattle.

"Oh," Jamie had replied, "that's okay. May I be excused now?"

As he wandered upstairs to his room, he counted on his fingers the number of moves they'd made that he could remember. Five. And there had been one other one, when he was just a baby, and two before that, that he knew of. They had lived in Maine and they had lived in Georgia, in northern New York and in western Idaho, and two places in Canada that he could hardly remember, except that in one of them, called Kenora, there were lots of Indians walking around.

When he was younger, Jamie would proudly announce at

school that his father was a troubleshooter; it sounded exciting and important, and besides, that's what Tom called himself. Actually, it was quite accurate too: Tom was a quality control expert on pulp and paper production, the best, Barbara said, that Troy-Battersea Ltd. had on its payroll. When there was a problem anywhere in T-B's extensive North American operation, Tom Benjamin usually got the call.

Sometimes, especially if it was during a school year, Tom would just fly off by himself and stay for as many weeks or months as it took to set things straight, getting home on weekends hit me could. But when a real overhaul was in order, the family went with him. Until Jericho, one place had seemed pretty much like another to Jamie. Oh, Atlanta was bigger and warmer and Kenora smaller and colder—that sort of thing—but they were just places to live in.

Instead of going directly into his room, Jamie detoured to the bathroom and sat there, far longer than he needed to, wondering if in Seattle he might finally make friends with some other children. If that happened—and who knows, it might, because he'd be in junior high out there, and more grown-up—then leaving Jericho and his strange comrades in the forest might not be so bad.

Jamie slipped into his room and closed the door quickly behind him. Then his heart jumped. Teddy was not where he'd left him that morning, sitting on the desk in front of the window. "Teddy?" There was a growing hint of panic in his voice. Where was he? What had they done with him? Jamie suddenly felt like he had to go to the bathroom all over again.

"Over here, kid," the deep, familiar voice said. "Behind the bed."

Jamie flung himself across the bed and came eye-to-button-eye with Teddy, who was stuffed down, looking very uncomfortable and picking dustballs from the worn, black flannel fur.

"Are you okay?" Jamie asked.

"To answer your first question first," Teddy replied, his voice a mixture of anger and relief, not to mention wounded dignity, "I was shoved down here by one Barbara Benjamin, your mother, when she cleaned your room this morning." Then the black eyes laughed mischievously. "Actually, it was worth it. She did her housework with all her clothes off today. Good-looking woman, your mother."

Jamie refused to acknowledge that, although he could feel his ears start to burn. Teddy was just being nasty again, taking it out on him because Barbara had tossed him on the floor. And besides, he didn't believe that Barbara would walk around the house naked. Oh, she used to, when he was just a really little kid, but she had stopped that in the last couple of years.

"She does have a nice one, Jamie," Teddy taunted.

"Dammit, Teddy, shut up! It's not true anyway; you just made it all up!"

"Maybe yes, maybe no," Teddy said. "Anyway, my young friend, tell me about your day. It gets awfully lonely for old Teddy, stuck in this room all day with nobody to talk to."

Jamie lay down on the bed and shifted Teddy so that they were facing one another. First he told him that they might be moving again, out to Seattle. All Teddy asked was when, and all Jamie told him was he didn't really know, but probably soon, in a month or so.

"Is that it?" Teddy asked. "Is that all you have to tell me?"

Jamie smiled. Now was his chance to get even with Teddy for all the teasing about Barbara, about her being naked. "Well," he said, drawing out the word, "I guess what happened in the woods today was kind of interesting." Then: "Nah, you probably wouldn't think so."

With that he rolled off the bed and went over to his desk, where he picked up a history textbook and began thumbing through the pages. He turned them ever so slowly, feeling Teddy's eyes trying to bore through the back of his head.

Finally the exasperated voice admitted defeat, "Okay, Jamie, you've made your point."

Jamie slammed the book closed triumphantly and dropped it back onto the desk. He was smiling happily when he resumed his position on the bed.

"So?" Teddy said.

"Just a second." Jamie went to the door and pressed his ear against it, listening for listeners. No, it was okay. They were still downstairs talking about Seattle.

"An old man fell down the hole today," Jamie said as he padded back to the bed. "I tried to stop him, but he fell down anyway. I saw him down there and he was dead. And then my friends came, and I guess they must have taken him some place down there, some other place I mean. It's okay, though, 'cause he was really dead."

When they were face-to face again, Jamie asked, "Did you ever see a dead person, Teddy?"

"Yes, I have."

"Did it bother you? Did it scare you I mean?"

"Nothing bothers me, you know that. Now please get on with the story."

Jamie eyed the door once more. If Tom or Barbara caught him talking to Teddy again, they might send Teddy away forever, like they'd almost done three years ago. If it hadn't been for good old Dr. Kelso, they might have too. They'd been very careful ever since, he and Teddy, but you could never be too careful. After about thirty seconds of hard listening, Jamie was satisfied that nobody was lurking in the hall, so he turned his attention back to Teddy.

"What do you think, Teddy?" he asked earnestly. "Should I tell somebody about it? Should I tell Tom and Barbara?"

"What's the point?" Teddy replied wearily. "The old bastard's dead and gone, and that's all there is to that. If you tell anybody, the cops'll come and question you and want to know why you didn't run right down to the police station and report it. They'll want to know what you were doing there in the woods in the first place. And if they start snooping around, who knows? They might even find your beasties."

"Don't call them beasties, Teddy. They're troglodytes, like I told you. Trogs. Like I showed you in the book."

Jamie hadn't realized he was half-shouting until Teddy barked, "Keep your goddamned voice down!"

Then he heard the footsteps in the hall and saw the doorknob begin to turn. Barbara stepped into the room, looking slightly curious, but mostly unhappy. Her blue eyes, almost precisely the same color and shape as Jamie's own, swept the room, then turned hard on Jamie and Teddy.

"Jamie," she demanded, "who are you talking to in here? Are you talking to the bear again, that pajama bag? Jamie, Jamie, I thought we had an understanding."

He bounded to his feet, placing himself strategically between her and Teddy. "Of course not, Barbara," he said, as if he had never heard anything quite so silly.

"Why would I talk to a bear?" As if to prove his point, he swept Teddy off the bed, back onto the floor where he'd found him earlier. Teddy's eyes blazed, and his mouth curled into a silent snarl. *Oh-oh,* Jamie thought, *am I ever going to get it for this. But first problems first.*

"I was just... uh... rehearsing, Barbara. For the school play." He could see that her expression hadn't changed, so he plunged on. "Didn't I tell you? I have a part in the school play. You know, for the end of the term.

"You are in a play?" she laughed. Then she caught herself and added, with appropriate gravity, "Well, Jamie, isn't that wonderful?"

So now they were even: he had given her a lie she could live with, and she had come back with phony praise. Fine with him. He had thrown her off the track again, and she was happy to be off that track. It wasn't the kind of relationship mothers and sons seemed to have in the books he read, but it suited him and it apparently suited her as well.

"Can I help you learn your lines?" she asked.

"Nah," he replied, watching for the relief to flicker into her eyes—which it did. "I can do it okay myself."

She closed the door quietly behind her. Jamie didn't have to listen for the retreating footsteps; she would leave him alone for a while now. He climbed across the bed, bracing himself for what he knew was coming.

"Teddy?"

"Go fuck yourself in the ass!"

"I'm really, really sorry," Jamie said, lifting Teddy out of the dusty corner one more time and brushing him off gently and straightening his left leg back into sitting position. He tried to hug Teddy, but he could feel the resistance, the blunt, dirty white ends of the little arms shoving him away. Jamie tried to avoid looking directly into the black button eyes. He knew what he would see there; he had seen it before.

"I had to do that," he explained when they were back on the bed. But Teddy faced away, and all Jamie could do was stroke him lovingly along the closed zipper and apologize some more and try to make the bear understand. "She'll take you away, Teddy. She'll take you and throw you in the garbage. She hates you, Teddy."

Then he lay back and closed his eyes, waiting for Teddy's anger to fade, as he knew it would. A few minutes later he gently rolled Teddy on his back, head on the pillow, and together they lay there, staring at the eating.

Finally, Teddy broke the silence. "You owe me one, Jamie. You have to make it up to me."

"Sure, Teddy. Anything."

"You know what I want you to do."

Yes, Jamie sighed deeply, he knew. He couldn't understand, at least not completely, what pleasure Teddy got out of it. And as for himself, well, it did feel kind of good while he was doing it, but afterwards he felt unhappy and confused and ashamed. So he'd pretend, as long as he could, that he didn't know what Teddy meant.

Teddy gave him a few seconds, then whispered in his ear, "Come on now, Jamie, you said 'anything?' Now why don't you get out the magazine or the book, if you'd prefer, and we'll get down to it, so to speak." Jamie still hesitated, and Teddy played his trump: "Or we could do it the way I like best anyway, couldn't we? Did I tell you how sexy-looking Barbara was today? Well, let's start with those beautiful tits. They—"

Jamie's hand was over his mouth. "No, Teddy," he sighed his defeat, "not that. I'll get the magazine."

"And take your clothes off too," Teddy ordered. "And put the light on."

Jamie slid his hand along between the mattress and box spring until his fingers found the thick, glossy magazine, the *Playboy* he'd found the previous fall while checking out the next-door neighbor's garbage late one night. Despite himself, despite his spoken and unspoken protest, coveting that much-tattered magazine sent a pleased title jolt into his groin. He slid it from its hiding place and opened it to the girl he liked the best, not the playmate, but the blond with the German name and the incredible tits.

Jamie's penis, still no bigger than his thumb and hairless as the day he was born, began to grow and throb, just at the thought of the German girl and her tits, and by the time he had his pants and undershirt yanked off, it was curving in a rigid arc toward his belly. With fumbling fingers, he got the magazine open and held it up, one-handed, so both he and Teddy could see. The other hand the left slid down his belly, almost as if it had its own mind, touched tentatively, then encircled and closed. The familiar sensations flooded through his body; his eyes felt terribly heavy, his throat full, his cheeks burning. His left hand began to move up and down, rhythmically, and he closed his eyes. He was getting close, so close.

Then Teddy screwed it all up.

"Do it. Do it. *Dooo* it, Jamie! Hurry, hurry!"

Jamie rolled away and sat on the edge of the bed. He released his penis and felt it start to sag and wither.

"I have to go to the bathroom," he said. He got shakily to his feet and started toward the door.

"We had it, Jamie," Teddy said, his voice thick and hoarse. "We really had it that time."

"Until you opened your big mouth, Teddy," he said coldly. He opened the closet door and took his yellow robe off the hook and struggled into it. "I'm going to the bathroom. To pee."

By the time he reached the bathroom door his anger with Teddy was just about gone. He couldn't stay mad at his best friend—his only friend really, until he found the trogs—for very long. In that way, they were very much alike.

FROM THE TIME he was a child in Hyannis, Massachusetts, Tom Benjamin had been forced to feign interest in baseball. His father, a small-time contractor who made a fair but not particularly good living replacing sidewalks and streets in a dozen Cape Cod towns, put on his Red Sox hat in April and rarely removed it until the team was mathematically eliminated from the pennant race, which, in the late Forties and throughout the Fifties, was often more early than late, Ted Williams notwithstanding. And every Sunday when the Sox were at home, Tom, his father, and his younger brother, Terry, would drive into father, and settle down with hot dogs and pop on the hard bench seats along the left field foul line.

Terry had actually gone on to play pro ball, getting as far as Soul Bend in the Three-I league before a shattered ankle sent him back home to the family business.

But the fact was that Tom Benjamin never liked baseball at all. He didn't like playing it, and he didn't like watching it, and he didn't like talking about it. The University of Minnesota had offered some respite, at least until his senior year when the old Washington Senators moved into Minneapolis, St. Paul—or Bloomington, to be precise—to become the new Minnesota Twins.

There was one thing Tom Benjamin knew, however, and it was simply that the best way to develop friendly business relationships with the people above and the people below was to have the ability to talk baseball, which was why he was lying on the floor, a couple of hand-hooked cushions propping up his head, digesting the last Brewers minutiae from the sports pages of the Milwaukee Journal. Was he a Brewers fan? You bet he was! He'd also been an Atlanta Braves fan when they'd lived there. And a Mets fan. And an Expos fan. In a few weeks, no doubt, he'd be cheering for the Seattle Mariners and saying wise things like, "For an expansion club they're not doing too bad, are they?" and "No problem that a third baseman and a good left-handed starter wouldn't solve."

He left Barbara looking at him. After fifteen, nearly sixteen, years of marriage, neither had to announce a need to talk. When they were younger, both before and after Jamie was born, they used to boast to one another and to their friends about how much in tune they were, about how beautifully they communicated their needs silently. Why was it that now Tom found this "magic" so irritating? And not just at this very moment. For some time.

"Yes, dear," he said, combining the words with a little sigh. The sigh was not lost, nor was it really meant to be.

"I was just thinking about moving again... and about

Jamie. I don't think he's well yet, like Dr. Kelso said he'd be. You know, what we've talked about before, about all the moving and everything not being too good for him."

"He seems okay now." Tom folded the paper and put it aside. She was obviously ready for a serious conversation and he knew he had to at least be polite and pretend to be interested. Jamie was like baseball to him. Always had been.

This could be a long one, he figured, so he tapped a Salem 100 out of the pack beside him and patted the pockets of his denim cutoffs until he detected the oval cylinder of the Bic lighter. The smoke tasted terrible, as it usually did by evening, thirty or thirty-five cigarettes removed from those first sweet, calming vapors of the morning. But he kept it going anyway, sacrificing pleasure for the need of a prop.

"He seems better now," she corrected, almost absently.

That was her way. In order not to sound anxious, she tried to make even her serious conversations sound casual. She was sewing the underarms back into one of Jamie's school shirts, and on this occasion, that was her prop. "But I don't really think he's okay. I think he's still talking to that... that bear."

No, Goddamn it, this was not going to be a long conversation. Not now, not after that. He retrieved the newspaper and held it up between them, pretending to read.

"Tom?"

"Look," he said, throwing the paper aside, "I am not going to get into another fucking conversation about Jamie and that fucking bear, do you understand? He doesn't talk to the bear, he's not crazy, and he's just like any other boy going into adolescence. Now drop it, Barbara. Just drop it!"

He rolled over on his stomach, punched out the remains of the last Salem cigarette, and lit the next.

"I just wish we didn't have to move again," she sighed, talking to the room generally in her husband's effective absence. "I wish sometimes he could have seen Dr. Kelso longer, or even that other psychiatrist none of us liked, Dr. Applegate—"

"Applebaum," he corrected, the sarcasm dripping. "His name was Applebaum.

And he was a psychologist, not a psychiatrist. And as far as I'm concerned, both of them were a waste of money."

CHAPTER THREE

THE JAMES K. POLK elementary school was built in the late Sixties, and in both structure and educational philosophy, it was a progressive school. Students sat in little groups doing projects and expressing themselves; and there were few teachers, but lots of "resource people."

Marian Lynde, however, was not a resource person. She was a teacher, trained in and for a time when sentences had to be broken down into their component parts, when two-plus-two was always four, and students were graded with As, Bs, and even Fs. She was not an old woman—forty-seven is not very old, except maybe to the very young—and she wasn't what one generally described as rigid, either. She'd started teaching in 1952, right after graduation, and called a temporary halt nine years later when Mikey, the first of her three sons, was born. She'd returned to her trade in 1976 at midterm, a few weeks after her husband died from a lingering cancer of the throat.

So Marian Lynde knew a lot about young boys. In fact, she sometimes imagined that she knew all about young boys. She'd watched two younger brothers grow to manhood and raised three sons of her own—not to mention the dozens who had passed through her classrooms in twelve years of teaching. Jamie Benjamin, she decided, was no worse than most—*stranger* than most, certainly, but not the strangest and not the worst. And she couldn't remember a brighter child, boy or girl.

Nor was she particularly shocked by the book in front of her. The women looked a little more tarty than she was accustomed to seeing in art books, and she wasn't entirely comfortable with women in chains or under apparent sexual menace, but she had no real inclination to blush, much less to recoil in horror. Times had changed, obviously, from the days when her husband brought *Playboy* home. She made a mental note to herself to take a look through *Penthouse* the next time Mikey left his copy lying around in the living room.

No, she decided, closing the book and turning back to the examinations she was supposed to be marking, she would not call Jamie Benjamin's mother and tell her what Jamie had brought to class for the free-reading period.

Yes, there was something quite odd about a twelve-year-old boy nonchalantly opening a book like *White Women* in front of a grade eight class and teacher, but she could find nothing particularly odd in a twelve-year-old boy wanting to look at those kinds of pictures. Even if the school term hadn't been almost over, she wouldn't have handled it any differently. Boys will be boys. Besides, Jamie was a good student, the best in his class, certain to win the math, history, English, and science prizes. He was one of those rare children who actually worked up to his potential, which, she knew from the intelligence test result was considerable, if not downright awesome. But she also knew that while Jamie would win all the prizes, he would never be valedictorian. The kids in the graduating class at Polk elected their valedictorian, and those kids did not like Jamie Benjamin.

The screech of the chalk on the blackboard behind her

did not make her wince. She was immune, long since conditioned and inured to it. However, because he obviously wanted her attention, she gave it to him. "Jamie, if you do that again, I'll give you another hundred lines. And don't think you're keeping me here, because I have to get these exams marked anyway."

"Yes, Mrs. Lynde," Jamie replied. The third blackboard was filled, and he was moving to the fourth. He'd already written the damn thing seventy-three times, but he looked back anyway, just to make sure he had the words right:

I WILL NOT BRING ADULT BOOKS TO SCHOOL

Damn Teddy. Jamie had told him this would happen, that he'd get caught and punished. How could he not get caught? But Teddy'd said not to worry, that if everything went according to plan, it would all be worth it. Teddy had said that Mrs. Lynde wouldn't do anything bad to him, and Jamie grudgingly admitted Teddy had been right about that.

But his arm ached, and his hand felt like it was turning into a claw. Flexing it, in case she caught him looking, he glanced over at Mrs. Lynde and noted happily that she had opened the book again and was turning the pages slowly. *Any time now*, he thought.

I WILL NOT BRING ADULT BOOKS TO SCHOOL

Oh, good, she's found it. She was at the page. In a few seconds she would ask him about it.

"Jamie...?"

"Yes, Mrs. Lynde."

"There's a page in here with, uh, with a woman's body cut out of it. Her head is here, but her body has been cut out. Do you know anything about that, Jamie?"

"It was like that when I got it, Mrs. Lynde." He spoke

matter-of-factly, very consciously not adding an "honest" to his statement.

He'd been ready for her question, and he lied well, although he tried to do so sparingly, saving his deceptions for when he really needed them the most. In fact, when Mrs. Lynde had asked him earlier how he got a book like *White Women* out of the library, he'd readily admitted to stealing it not to keep but to look at and then smuggle back. No, Jamie only lied when he really had to. Like when he was telling his mother the things he sensed she wanted to hear.

He hadn't stopped working. Three more lines to go.

Mrs. Lynde studied the defiled page again and concluded that yes, anybody could have done it. From all the dates stamped on the card, *White Women* was apparently a popular item over at Jericho Public & Lending Library. Besides, the cutout work was very precise, far more likely the work of an adult's hand than a child's. She'd take Jamie's word for it, anyway.

Jamie was finished. Wiping his hands on his jeans he sauntered over to Mrs. Lynde's desk and stood in front of her, waiting to be recognized and dismissed.

"Okay, Jamie," she said, looking up from the book and flashing a smile that said everything was all evened up. "Just wipe the boards clean and you can go."

"What about the book?" he asked. "I have to take it back."

She was ready for that. "I'm going past the library," she said. "I'll take it back. I want to talk to Miss Livingstone about it, tell her about the page."

Jamie hung his head and made himself look very worried. Mrs. Lynde took the bait. "Don't worry," she said kindly, almost reaching over the desk to pat his hand, but then deciding against it, on the grounds that it might embarrass him further. "I won't tell her where it came from—at least I won't tell her if you make me a solemn promise, right here and now, that you won't go around bragging about what you did. And I also want you to promise that you won't ever do it again. Do I have your word?"

"Yes, Mrs. Lynde," he said softly, adding a little tremor to his voice for effect.

This time she didn't respond to his tricks.

"Okay, Jamie," she said, "you can go. After you clean the blackboards."

"Well?" Teddy demanded. He was sitting in the old corduroy armchair that had been part of Jamie's parents' first living room set, the one they'd had before Jamie was born.

Jamie was on the floor in front of Teddy, sitting cross-legged and looking up at him.

"It was no big deal," Jamie said.

"But the plan worked?"

"Some of it worked. All of the first part worked."

"Okay," Teddy sighed impatiently, "let's get on with it. And don't leave anything out. I want to hear all the details."

Jamie ran through all the stuff that had happened at school as quickly as he could. He knew that Teddy had very little interest in that, and the bear did not interrupt until Jamie got to the part about the library.

"What was Miss Livingstone wearing today?"

"I was going to tell you that. First, I—"

"I want to know now," Teddy demanded.

Jamie had to think for a moment. If he told Teddy the truth, that Miss Livingstone had worn a straight black skirt and an ordinary, light-blue blouse, and that she had her glasses on all the time, and that her hair was up in a bun, Teddy'd just go into one of his sour moods and stay that way for the rest of the night.

Teddy was always unreasonable when it came to Miss Livingstone; he kept insisting that she was the most beautiful woman in Jericho. Frankly, Jamie could not understand what his friend saw in her. To him, she was a crotchety, mean old lady—not as old as that frigging Miss Oliphant, not even as old as Barbara, but old, and who was always following him around the library, spying on him, telling him to keep quiet, even when he wasn't doing anything wrong.

Besides, she was that rotten Abergail's aunt, and Abergail always seemed more rotten when she was with Miss Livingstone.

Once, in the park, Jamie had eavesdropped on a group of older boys talking about Miss Livingstone. One of them said that she was "queer" and the others had all laughed a little bit; and then another boy claimed that his father had said that too. Jamie hadn't known what "queer" meant, except for "odd and strange" and maybe "weird," and when he'd asked Teddy about it, the bear had just said: "That's bullshit, Jamie. Bullshit."

Oh yes: Teddy. "She had on this silky blouse," he began, deciding that he might as well make it good, "and when she bent over, you could see her tits. And her nipples were really hard, Teddy..." Teddy really got excited about nipples; Jamie always had to include anything about nipples in his stories. "And she was wearing tight white pants, Teddy, and it didn't look like she had any underwear on. And her hair was hanging down her back. She really looked sexy."

"Did she touch herself?" Teddy was breathing hard.

"No. I... uh... I mean I'm not sure. Wait! She did touch herself down there once."

"What did she look like then? Did it make her happy? Did her face get all red?"

Jamie just wanted to tell the story. It was tough enough trying to make up details as he went along. Why did Teddy have to be such a pain sometimes? All that really happened was that Mrs. Lynde had gone into the library and asked to speak with Miss Livingstone personally. Jamie crouched down in the bushes, had watched all that from the window. And he'd seen Miss Livingstone come out of her office, and Mrs. Lynde, whose back was to Jamie, had said something and handed over the book.

"Which boy?" Miss Livingstone had asked.

Mrs. Lynde must have said that she didn't want to say who it was, because Jamie heard Miss Livingstone reply that she knew anyway, that it was "the Benjamin brat" who, to her way of thinking, wasn't "quite right in the head." But Mrs. Lynde had kept her promise and hadn't said anything to Miss Livingstone after that except that she had to go.

When Mrs. Lynde had gone, Miss Livingstone had stood there clutching the book, and Jamie noticed that she was biting her lip and that her knuckles had gone all white. Then she'd opened the book and flipped through rapidly, stopping finally at *the* page. Then her face had got all red and her eyes had gone all cold and mean, and even though she'd whispered it, Jamie heard her words. "Perverted, disgusting little bastard!"

However: "She opened the book, Teddy, and her face got all red and hot looking. Then she went back into her office, and I went around and looked in that window too, like you said to do."

Miss Livingstone had placed the book on her desk and stood a few feet away, looking at it as if it was a snake or a spider. After a few minutes—at least it had seemed that long to Jamie—she'd opened it to *the* page again. Then she'd reached into a drawer and taken out the envelope. She'd started biting her lip again, and she was pushing her hands through her hair, and some of it had come loose and was falling in front of her face. Then she'd started walking very fast in short little circles.

"She took the picture, Teddy, and she held it up and looked at it really close, and then she undid some more buttons on her blouse and put her hand inside, and she was rubbing her tits—you know, breathing hard and everything."

Miss Livingstone had taken the picture—the naked, kneeling woman from the book with her own face pasted on it—and crumpled it up. Then she'd opened the ball of paper and torn it into little shreds and thrown the pieces into the wastebasket. All the time she'd been muttering "creep" and "pervert" and "disgusting little bastard." Finally, she'd hurled the whole book into the wastebasket and stomped out of the room, slamming the door behind her. Jamie had heard water running and guessed she must be in her private bathroom.

"She was really sexed up, Teddy. I could tell. Then she had to go to the bathroom, and I bet you I know what she did in there..."

"She was touching herself!" Teddy said triumphantly.

"I'm sure she did, Teddy. I know she did."

"Then what happened?"

The library caretaker, Mr. Wasilewsky, had grabbed Jamie by the shirt collar and yanked him away from the window, yelled "No-good-son-of-a-bitch-kid" at him and aimed a kick at his ass that Jamie just managed to avoid.

"I had to leave, Teddy. I saw the caretaker coming, and I got scared, so I snaked along the side of the building and got away."

The bear sighed.

CHAPTER FOUR

Because he was a good cop, and because the Morley disappearance was his case, David Bentley tried to keen his mind on his work, which was to command the point position, seven men on his left and seven on his right, of the volunteer search team. But he was distracted by this place, this strange, rectangular clearing all covered with grassy hummocks. Even stranger than the place actually was the fact that he'd never been there before, either as child or man. And, he was certain, neither had any of the men who were with him today, marching from end to end.

Whately's Copse. The name was hardly used any more, but he imagined that the legend remained, that each new generation of Jericho parents was still warning each new generation of Jericho children to stay away from there. It was probably phrased a lot more scientifically now, though, with "seismic activity" and "unstable crust" replacing "bogeyman."

The world had grown up a lot in David's thirty years and so had Jericho; the small town of his early childhood was now a city of eighty-five heady pace. But some things never changed. Where else in the world would more than a dozen men take a day off from work—or play—to spend their time traipsing through much and underbrush to help out the police? Not many places, he figured. It made him feel a little proud.

"Hey," he heard, somewhere not far to his left, "I think I've found something!" Hank Denmond, the twenty-two-year-old kid who was already on his way to his first million thanks to a car restoration business he'd founded two years before, was holding something high in the air with his right hand, pointing at it excitedly with his left. David joined the growing circle of men and reached out his hand. They certainly looked like an old man's glasses, David thought, just the kind that he'd have expected somebody like the Reverend Morley to wear. The lenses were almost round, the frames of worn-thin metal, and there was a safety pin securing the right armature to the frame. The plastic earpieces were well chewed, and a too-heavy silver chain still hung from them.

"Anybody recognize these?" David asked, holding up the glasses. From the corner of his eye he saw a gray-haired man begin to move in closer. His name was Labonte and, like his father before him, he ran the two-chair barbershop just a block up Main Street from where it crossed Madison to form Jericho's central intersection.

"They're his," Labonte said without hesitation. "He was wearing them just last week when he came in for a haircut."

Then somebody else said, "Hey, Dave, I think you'd better have a look at this." In the top of the closest mound, and the largest in the clearing, was a hole. A man, whose name David could not recall, stepped gingerly to the crest of the mound and dropped to his knees. He brushed at the lip of the hole with his hands and announced, "I think something slid down here."

"Can you see anything?" David asked, joining the man on the mound and copying his prone position.

"No. Too dark."

"Hank," David turned to Denmond, "could you run out to

the road and get the big flashlight out of the cruiser?" He fished the keys out of his pocket and tossed them. Denmond fielded them easily and loped away from the gathering. "Hank!" Denmond stopped and turned his head. "There's a coil of rope in the trunk," David said. "Can you get that too?"

Denmond waved and disappeared into the trees.

"Stupid old man," David muttered.

When he was just a child, nine or maybe ten, one of the boys in his class, Danny Trowbridge, had gone into these woods on a dare one black Halloween night. David and the other kids had waited by the road, laughing and talking and shouting at Danny. They thought he was far inside the trees, and that in a little while he'd come out and collect the $1.76 he'd earned from them for his feat of courage. But an hour passed, and there was no Danny, David and the others talked about going in after Danny, and they shouted for him and whistled and even lit a big bonfire so that he could see his way out; but they were too terrified to go in for him.

After midnight David stood in the doorway of the police station, tears in his eyes—and fear—and blurted out to his father, who was then chief of police, about Danny Trowbridge. All that night and all the next day the police and the men from the town searched, but neither Danny nor any trace of him was ever found. The hole wasn't there then, or if it was, nobody ever came across it. After a while, everybody gave up. There was no point in dragging the quarry pond because in some places it was hundreds of feet deep. But Danny's father and his older brother did it anyway. They hauled a rowboat by hand through the overgrown (even in early November) woods, and for a week or more they dragged. They returned every weekend after that until the pond was frozen over. Danny's body was never found and that had been twenty years ago.

And, David recalled, Danny might not have been the first person to disappear forever in these woods. One blustering night, about a month after Danny had ventured into Whately's Copse, David's father had recounted the local legend. He didn't believe in it, of course, he made that very clear. But it made sense to David. At least when he was nine or ten-years-old.

The land had belonged to a family named Whately, a very strange family by his father's handed-down account. They had come to Wisconsin from the East Coast—some said Rhode Island, some said New Hampshire—sometime in the 1870s. Of the two hundred acres of land they purchased, about one hundred were woodlot. By the turn of the century, Old Man Whately, who was by then a very old man indeed, had, with the help of his five sons, cleared all but the twenty-five acres that still remained, and which was thereafter known as Whately's Copse. The central clearing, so the story went, was natural. Jericho had just been a farming village then, with a population of less than two thousand, and much of the modern city would be built on the land where the Whately Holstein herd once grazed. One night in 1911, a vicious February night when the temperature dropped to forty-eight below, the Whately house and barn had both burned to the ground. The charred corpses of the cattle were found, but not those of the Whately family. Not a sign. Apparently, after the fire they had just packed up what they could salvage and had left.

Those were the facts, the bare bones. But there was more.

Hank Denmond had to say it twice before David really heard him, "You want me to go down?"

Almost back in the present, Bentley reached out automatically for the rope, took it out of Denmond's hand, and recalling the emergency-measures-training course he'd taken when he joined the force, quickly fashioned a body sling around himself. Without him having to give the order, five or six of the men formed half of a tug-of-war team behind him.

David was only a foot or so below ground level when his

nostrils seized and his eyes filled with water and swelled into slits. He was gasping audibly, trying to suck enough air through his mouth to see him through. He looked up into half-a-dozen concerned faces but smiled weakly and waved the flashlight to indicate he was okay.

"Allergies," he explained. "Mold. Wet down here. 'S'all right. Just look around." His feet were against one slippery wall; then in a controlled fall, he dropped in foot-and-a-half to two-foot stages to the bottom. He guessed it was about twenty feet below the surface.

"Anything?" A voice wafted down from the circle of light above.

"Don't know. Don't think so. Just a minute." Even the big flashlight didn't make it a hell of a lot brighter down there. The moist black earth of the walls and floor seemed to absorb most of the light, returning virtually none in reflection. Before he even started looking for signs of the Reverend Morley, David noted the shape of the pit. The bottom was flat and about as wide across as the pit was deep; it was such a perfect cone, this hole, that for a fleeting moment David was asking himself if it could possibly be manmade. No. Ridiculous. He shook off the notion.

"Any sign of our man down there?" That was Hank's voice.

"Not a thing," David shouted back. "All I can see is what looks like animal scratchings in the dirt." He squatted and began to run his fingertips over the surface of the floor, scooping up handfuls every so often and letting the dirt sift through his fingers.

"Ohhh shit!" he yelled suddenly.

"What?" Three or four voices formed a chorus from above.

"Shit," David said with revulsion. "Some kind of animal shit." He tried to shake it off his fingers; some of it came off and some of it didn't. Well, he was goddamned if he was going to wipe it on his uniform, even if the department did pick up the cleaning bills. He rubbed the worst of the rest of it into the dirt, careful not to acquire any more in the process.

"What kind of animal would live down there?" Hank Denmond yelled down to him.

Before David could answer one of the other men did it for him. "Badger."

"So that's where they all go after the Ohio State game," somebody laughed. "Seen any of your old teammates down there, Davey?"

Then everybody was laughing. Thirteen years ago, David Bentley, carrying Jericho's honor with him, had gone off to the University of Wisconsin on a football scholarship. After two years of sitting on the bench, he decided that he just wasn't cut out to be an outside linebacker after all. He returned home in the fall of his junior year, and against his father's wishes but not his orders, he joined the police force. For lack of a better target, David took the whole town's blame every time Wisconsin suffered another Saturday afternoon drubbing.

"Fuck you," he shouted back.

"Don't take it so hard, Davey," one of them said. "Just think: what if you'd gone to Illinois?"

This time, as best he could under the breathing conditions, he joined in the laughter. Then, very suddenly, nothing seemed very funny anymore. He felt an overpowering hatred for this place. There was something—no, more than one thing terribly wrong about it. Evil? No, it was just ugly. No, not evil. It was just because he'd been half-remembering all that stuff about the Whatelys. Nevertheless his skin was crawling, and he had the overwhelming need to be under a boiling hot shower, scrubbing himself, scrubbing off all this stinking, cloying filth. He forced himself to take one more look around. There had to be tunnels, two of them. He turned his eyes around again, no, three. Running off into the walls right at floor level.

Reluctantly he crawled toward the nearest, playing the beam of his light around the circumference, estimating the opening to be eighteen-to-twenty-inches in diameter.

He poked the flashlight in its own length, plus the length of his forearm, but the tunnel ended abruptly in what appeared to be a right-angle turn. He could see maybe eight or ten feet into the second tunnel, but it too curved-downward this time. For a reason that he could not explain, David did not want to peer down that third tunnel. It seemed to be no different from the other two, at least not in the size or shape of the opening, but David had the sensation of pushing his luck.

For Christ's sake, he told himself, *you're thirty years old and you're a man and you're a cop; you're just being an asshole.* The reproach didn't help much, but he decided he had to do his duty as he saw I especially with all those witnesses up there.

"Unnhhh!"

"What? What's going on? Davey?"

"Nothing. Nothing." His heart was pumping and his throat felt full, constricted.

"Nothing. Get me out of here."

On the surface once more, David avoided the curious eyes of the men surrounding him.

"Didn't fall in here," he muttered. "I guess we'll have to try the quarry." Then he looked at his watch and at the fading, late-evening sun. "Tomorrow," he said. "As many of you as can make it tomorrow, can you meet me out by the road where we came in this afternoon? Jerry, can you tow your boat along? I think we can carry it in between us."

The men began to drift away, some individually and others in groups of two and three. When they were all gone, David sat down on a hummock, unaware that it was the same hummock the Reverend Morley had plunked down on two days before to study the cedar waxwing, and looked toward the hole. God Jesus, it felt good to be out of there. He looked up to see Hank staring at him quizzically from the edge of the clearing. David managed what he hoped looked like a rueful smile and waved the young man away. He wanted to go home alone tonight and talk to nobody about the hole and the tunnels.

Besides, he was no longer sure that he'd actually seen those terrible yellow eyes.

WHEN HE WAS sure the policeman had gone, Jamie hand-over-handed himself down the rope and stood in the dying twilight, looking intently toward the hole. He had arrived unnoticed a couple of hours before and climbed up to his perch to watch. And listen. So Old Morley wasn't down there? They hadn't found anything down there. But the cop, when he came up, he was scared, wasn't he? Even from that far away and with the light not as good, Jamie could tell that the cop had been scared. But he couldn't have seen them, could he? Or he'd have shot them or something. Sure.

Jamie smiled to himself and whistled a little tune that he'd either heard someplace or made up, he didn't recall which. Oh yes, now he remembered; it was what old Morley had been humming just before he died. The sun was almost gone now, the woods dressed for the evening in shades of gray.

"Good night," he said into the hole. "I won't be here for a couple of days. When all those men stop coming, then I'll come back. Good night."

CHAPTER FIVE

THE BENJAMINS HAD ARRIVED in Jericho in mid-August of 1979, August the 17th to be precise. And on August the 19th, at about ten thirty in the morning, Jamie had received his first beating. The boy's name was Freddy Hoekstra, and although he was going into the same eighth grade as Jamie, he was a year and a half older, and his voice had already changed. He had real muscles and the fuzzy, but dark, beginnings of a mustache.

Jamie had been sitting alone on one of three playground swings, whistling to himself, kicking just enough to maintain a four- or five -foot arc, when out of nowhere this man-boy was looming over him. What the hell did Jamie think he was doing, sitting on Freddy's girlfriend's swing, anyway? Jamie hadn't answered back. Experience had taught him that sometimes when you don't answer back, you don't get hit.

He'd glanced to his left to see the girl friend's smirking face, with its washed-out blue eyes tamed by a frizzle of blond hair, almost as blond as his own. He hadn't wanted to look at the boy; sometimes when you looked at guys like that, especially if you looked them in the eye, they'd hit you.

The girl had tits—little tits like half-lemons, but tits. He'd been looking at those tits when the blow came. It was a hard punch. It came out of nowhere and caught Jamie flush on the left side of his face. It lifted him out of the seat and sent him flying backwards onto the back-hard dirt.

Freddy had stood over him, fists clenched, a wicked sadistic smile on his face.

"When I say move, shitface, I mean move." Jamie had just looked at him blankly and pretended to clear his head. Sometimes that worked; if you made like you were hurt, really hurt, sometimes they didn't hit you again. Jamie had stood up with his back to the man-boy, and dabbed at the blood that was trickling out of his left nostril. He'd waited for the punch to the back of his head, the one that would send him on his way, but it never came. Only a shove. "Go on," Freddy had said, pushing him again, "Get out of here, shitface. Get your ass out of here. And if I ever catch you on my girlfriend's swing again, I'll really give it to you." Jamie heard the girl giggle as he walked away.

Jamie never returned to the playground again, and he never saw the girl or boy again until school started, which was also when he finally learned their names. Freddy and Christina. She even lived on Jamie's street. On the third day of school, with about thirty kids watching, Freddy beat him up again, while the lemon-tits girl giggled.

Jamie never said anything to anybody about it. He had learned years before that complaining never did any good, that nobody really cared anyway. Oh once, back in Glen's Falls, the teacher had caught a bunch of boys beating him up and they were all given detentions for a month. After that everybody had left him alone for the rest of the school year, at least until the next-to-last day. He'd gone into the washroom and was peeing when all the lights went out. Something woolly and foul-tasting was shoved in his mouth, and he was wrestled to the floor by how many hands he didn't know. He was blindfolded too, and he could feel his clothes being stripped off. Everything. In the darkness—he had never known whether or not the lights had been turned back on he heard nasty, giggling laughter but no words, no identifiable voices. When he had realized, however many minutes later, that he was once more alone, he'd lifted the blindfold and spat out the sweat sock that had been his gag; his clothes had been distributed in the four urinals, piss-soaked, and his shoes in one stall, filled with feces.

No, he never told on other kids—not even that time—and after a while they pretty much left him alone. And he never ever fought back. And he never ever talked back. He didn't cry and he didn't beg and he didn't threaten to get even. The truth was that Jamie, at least as far as he could tell, didn't mind much any more. He knew his place, and he accepted it. As the years passed he couldn't really remember what had happened in Georgia and what had happened in Canada. Faces blurred. Events blurred. Places blurred.

And when they moved again, to Seattle, Freddy and Christina and Abergail and all of the rest of Jericho, Wisconsin, would blur too. Only six more days of school, then maybe, in Seattle, in high school, things would be better.

"Hey, douchebag!" Jamie refused to look up. He knew it was Freddy Hoekstra, on the other side of the street, walking to school with Christina, whose tits were still like lemons. Jamie didn't know what "douchebag" meant, but he assumed it was disgusting, like "shitface." He kept walking, head down, pretending he hadn't heard.

"Hey, you! Douchebag! I'm talking to you!" Jamie heard Christina's stupid giggling. "You got in shit again, eh? You brought that dirty book to school, you dumb dork. Too bad you got to do it with a book, too bad you haven't got a girl..."

"Oh, Freddy, don't be gross!" She giggled some more.

Only six more days, Jamie told himself. Deliberately he slowed his pace and didn't pick it up again until he saw Freddy and Christina round the corner. He wished they were dead. Well, maybe not dead. Badly wounded would do.

On the sidewalk in front of him a bicycle lay on its side. Abergail's bicycle. He looked up. Abergail's house, Abergail's and Miss Livingstone's. He looked around. No Abergail. He looked around again, just to be sure. He reached down and lifted the bike onto its wheels, holding it up by the handlebars with his left hand so that he could inspect it. It was beautiful. All red and silvery chrome. French, he knew. A ten-speed. Expensive, hundreds of dollars. Much better than his own bike, but right now anything was better than his own bike. Tom and Barbara probably wouldn't let him ride it again until they were in Seattle, if then. That frigging Miss Oliphant.

Jamie stroked the gleaming metal, warm to the touch in the June morning sun, and then, dreamily, straddled it. The handlebar grips felt so good in his hands, and he closed his eyes for a moment or two, just letting the whole pleasure of the experience wash through him.

Suddenly he sensed someone nearby, and in his scramble to get off and away, he let the bicycle topple heavily and noisily back onto the concrete of the sidewalk. His right foot got caught up in it somehow, and he sprawled, scraping skin off the heel of his left hand as he tried to block his fall.

"If that bike is broken, you little creep, you'll wish you'd never been born!" Abergail shrieked!

Jamie scuttled away as the bike was angrily snatched up. The girl looked down her sunburned nose at him.

More than Freddy, more than just about anybody, Abergail Buhl made him afraid. She was different from the other kids; not in the way that he was different, but different. He had never heard her laugh at anything that wasn't, to his mind, cruel. (Sometimes, when he was talking to Teddy, he'd call her "Cruel Buhl.") She was laughing now. She had examined her bike and, having assured herself that it was undamaged, she just stood and laughed. It stung him as he crouched —no, cowered—there, half on the sidewalk, half on the grassy boulevard.

"You're lucky, funny person. You're really *lucky,*" she sneered, wetting her finger and rubbing at some spot on the bicycle seat that Jamie hadn't even seen. She set the bike down lightly and stood over him, her legs apart, as if daring him to even try to look up the short, pleated skirt she was wearing.

Instead he scuttled a few feet farther away. But he still wondered if Teddy was right when they'd talked about Abergail, if she really did touch herself down there. The thought confused him, and he could feel his brain clouding up. He stood and, not bothering to brush himself, turned his back on her and walked away. After twenty or thirty steps he realized he was heading for home, not school, and even though she was still standing there, he turned, crossed the street and, head down, passed her.

"Yeah, funny person, you stay over on that side of the street from now on," she shouted at him. "Or I'll tell my Aunt Margaret, and she'll call your mother, and you'll never get your bike back. And you know something else, creepy Jamie Benjamin? Some day they're going to come for you, the men in the white coats, and they're going to take you away and put you somewhere, somewhere with rubber walls. You know who says? I say. And Aunt Margaret says..."

The farther away he got, the louder she shouted. He could feel people standing in doorways, watching him and listening to her. He could feel people coming around from their backyards. He wanted to put his hands over his ears, to block her out. What he really wanted to do was run back and grab her by that perfect red hair and smash her face into the sidewalk. The blood was pounding in his face, and his ears almost crackled under the heat of the blush. But he kept on walking.

"Aunt Margaret knows, funny person. She knows. She knows it was you who sent the picture."

For the first time since he'd left the house that morning, Jamie felt himself smile. Teddy would be so happy when he told him.

CHAPTER SIX

SHE WAS, Jamie believed, just about the most beautiful girl he'd ever seen.

And there she was, standing in his backyard, asking him if he was Jamie. He couldn't even speak right away. He nodded instead.

"Well," she said, showing perfect white teeth, "I'm Sandy. Sandy O'Reilly. I'm going to be staying with you for a while unless it isn't okay with you, of course."

She knelt down beside him on the grass. "Your mother hi... your mother asked me to stay with you for the next week or so while she and your father are in Seattle. They're looking for a new home for you."

He didn't like to be talked down to, not usually, anyway, but he didn't let on to her. Her lips looked so soft, and she had such pretty eyes. Seattle? Oh yes, what they were talking about last night. Yes, they were moving to Seattle. He realized, with shame he'd never remembered feeling before, that he had a grasshopper in his right hand and a closed jar full of them on the ground beside his knee.

"Bugs," he mumbled. "For the toads and the snakes. My terrarium." That felt stupid too. At that very moment he didn't want to be young enough to have a terrarium and toads and snakes, and he especially didn't want to be young enough to be grubbing around the backyard on his hands and knees. He put the last grasshopper in the jar and, leaving it on the ground, he stood. Sandy's hand went out to help him up, but he pretended not to see it.

He scrubbed his own bug-filthy hand against his jeans and, seeing that hers was still stretched out toward him, he tentatively reached for it. Oh, it was so soft and warm, and small, not much bigger than his own. Lovely warmth started in his belly and flowed all through him.

"I'm Jamie," he said finally, speaking softly.

He didn't know what to do next. His hand was still in hers, and he didn't want that to end. It was like... holding hands. So that's what it felt like, so that's why other people, other kids, did it. It felt wonderful, not dirty or sexy or anything, but warm and comfortable. He looked away from the clasped hands, up into her face, to see if it was all right. She was still smiling, so it must be okay. What a beautiful smile.

"Hello!" Barbara, damn her, was pushing out through the screen door, and Sandy was turning toward the voice. Jamie felt her hand slip away and her attention transfer. He stuck his hand deep into his pocket and began to check the grass for more bugs.

"I'm Barbara Benjamin," Barbara said, reaching out her own hand to Sandy. Sandy took it, but only briefly. Jamie was instantly happy that Sandy didn't touch and hold hands that way with everybody, the way she did with him.

"Hi. I'm Sandy O'Reilly. We spoke on the phone."

"I thought you might be. Won't you come in? I have some coffee on." The two women walked side by side toward the door, and Jamie began to follow. "No, Jamie," his mother said, "you stay out here for a little while. Sandy and I have some things to discuss."

Jamie tried not to look at Sandy; he didn't want her to see what he knew must be showing in his face. But be couldn't help it. And he knew—he just *knew* that she understood what he was feeling. Her eyes were saying, *I'm sorry, Jamie; I wouldn't treat you that way; I like you, Jamie.* Then she smiled, and so did he. As the door started to close behind the two women Jamie saw Sandy's hand wave conspiratorially at him, from behind her back so Barbara wouldn't see. He smiled again and waved back.

🐻

"I HOPE he doesn't cause you any trouble, Sandy."

"Oh, I'm sure he won't," Sandy replied. *What a strange way to open a conversation with someone you've just met*, she thought. She didn't like to go by first impressions, but what they told her in this case was first there was trouble in the Benjamin household, it wasn't all because of Jamie. Was the place always this tidy and clean? Did it always smell of lemon oil and forest glade kinds of air freshener? Were people allowed to actually sit at that dining room table?

Sandy noticed the indentations her sneakers had made in the thick, off-white carpet, and she was actually asking herself if she should try to smooth them out while Barbara was in the kitchen getting the coffee. She was even apprehensive about actually rocking in the chair she had chosen— chosen solely because it was the only thing in the room that looked hospitable to the human bum. Mentally she added everything in that living room, especially the atmosphere, to her list of things that she would not have in her own future home.

"I hope you're right," Barbara said, emerging from the kitchen with delicate bone-china cups, creamer, and sugar bowl on a silver ray. "But I think it's only fair to warn you Jamie is sometimes a... uh... difficult boy."

45

Does she want me to stay here or doesn't she? What's she trying to do? I met Jamie, and he's no monster. He's shy and polite. What does she mean by difficult? Should I ask? No, she'll tell me and I'll listen and then after Jamie and I are alone for a while I'll make up my own mind. But I'd better say something.

"Psychology is my major, Mrs. Benjamin, as I told you on the phone. If I'm accepted, I'll be going into graduate school next year. I know that doesn't mean all that much,"—*better I say it before she thinks it*—"but it should help a little." *Better try to change the subject.* "How long did you say you and your husband would be away?"

Barbara's coffee sat untouched, making Sandy feel guilty that hers was almost gone.

"A week, perhaps ten days," Barbara said. "Tom—my husband—is going to a new job out there."

"Yes." Sandy already knew that. She even knew what Tom Benjamin did for a living—from the phone conversation earlier that day, when Barbara had called the college placement service and Sandy, filling in time until her real summer employment began July 5, had taken both the call and the job.

"Anyway, about Jamie," Barbara resumed, apparently obsessed with the need to get all of it in the open. "He has problems... uh... relating to people. Especially other kids. You won't see any other kids around here, so don't worry about it. And I wouldn't ask him about it either, but that's up to you, of course."

The hell it is, Sandy thought. "Has he seen anybody about... you know... these problems, Mrs. Benjamin?"

"A psychiatrist in Atlanta and a psychologist up in Maine. A few years ago. I don't really know whether it helped or not," The formality was starting to break down a little, and Sandy sensed that this woman, this perfectly coiffed and made-up and dressed woman in front of her was more than just some uptight bitch mother. She was worried about Jamie. Very worried.

Ah, Sandy thought, not willing to go soft on this woman just yet, *but how much of the problem is Jamie's and how much of it is yours?*

"Please don't misunderstand me, Sandy—and please call me Barbara, it makes me feel not as old—I've just somehow lost touch with the boy. I don't know when it happened or how it happened but even when he was a little baby, still in diapers, he was so... so strange. I'd pick him up and hold him, and he'd push me away—no, that's not true: he just wouldn't hold me back..." She was biting her lip, and for a moment Sandy thought she was going to cry. Then Barbara turned her head, and she was looking at Sandy again, her composure had apparently fully returned.

"I'm sorry," she said finally. "It just bothers me some times more than others. Can I get you more coffee?" Not waiting for an answer she replaced the cup carefully on the tray and went back out to the kitchen.

Jesus, Sandy thought, *what have I got myself in for? If the husband's as bad as she is, I'm going to fake a migraine attack and go back to the phones at the placement office. What does this poor kid do, anyways? Does he throw fits? Does he set fire to things? Does he pull the wings off flies?*

She heard the screen door open and bang shut, and she assumed it was Jamie's, but when Barbara returned from the kitchen there was a slim, well-dressed man with her.

"Sandy, this is my husband, Tom. Tom, this is Sandy O'Reilly, who's going to stay with Jamie." Tom Benjamin covered the space between them quickly and fluidly, taking her hand for just the right amount of time and exerting just the right amount of pressure. Up close he looked quite young, the gray hairs in his well-groomed sideburns making the face look even younger. He was not, as Sandy had first thought, handsome. He was more like a "good-looking guy" of her own generation. But he was thirty-five or forty—had to be—and that was too old to be a good-looking guy. His face had no character. Yes, that was it: no character. The mouth smiled, but the eyes did not. *He'll be a very handsome man*, Sandy thought, *when he gets a few lines*.

"Tom," Barbara said, forcing her smile, "I've just been warning Sandy here about the dangers of babysitting with 'the Benjamin brat.'"

Tom hadn't liked that, not at all. But he'd put on his own smile and tried to pick up the spirit of the conversation his wife was promoting. "He can be a trial, all right," he offered, shaking his head mechanically. "But don't you worry, Sandy, he's not nearly as bad as Barbara tries to let on. She's just hedging her bets, you know making you expect the worst so you'll be grateful when it never happens. Jamie's okay, he's just going through a difficult stage, that's all."

Tom excused himself gracefully and went upstairs, presumably to change out of his suit and tie. Barbara's eyes followed him and didn't return to Sandy until she was sure her husband was out of listening range. Even then she whispered, leaning forward with enough melodramatic urgency to prompt Sandy to do the same. Barbara licked the dryness from her lips.

"Tom doesn't understand Jamie," she said, eyes flicking toward the stairs. Sandy watched her trying to compose the right words, to avoid saying anything stupid. "Call it a mother's instinct-though, hysterical sounding. God knows, I've never thought much of myself as a mother, at least not by my own mother's standards or my younger sister's—but I don't think my son is just 'going through a stage.' If he is, then he always has been, There's never been a time when—"

A noise upstairs startled her. But, satisfied that it was only the shower running, she resumed.

"There has never been anything but stages. The psychiatrists gave us explanations, but—and you're the first person

I've ever said this to, Sandy—I have my own feelings. Jamie is different. He's beautiful and he's bright and he's a lot of other things that seem good and desirable. But there's something missing, Sandy. People get to know him, and they don't like him. Other kids don't like him right away. They... they seem to *know* something. Older people take longer, but they don't' like him either. Tom won't admit it, but he doesn't like his son. And, God help me, neither do I."

Exhausted, she slumped back into the leather chair, and her left hand went up to shade her eyes. She sighed deeply. "I'm sorry, Sandy," she said in a weary, old-woman voice. "And I'm ashamed. I guess I told you because after next week I'll likely never see you again, and I won't have to look at you and know that you know."

Sandy let a few agonizing minutes pass, as many as she could stand, before beginning to fidget out of her chair. Her body ached from the tension. She felt as if she'd just done an hour of calisthenics, except that it was not the righteous pain that follows' good exercise. Blearily she collected her red canvas shoulder bag and headed toward the door, unescorted.

"I guess," the woman in the leather chair said to Sandy's retreating back, "you won't be here tomorrow."

Damn it, Sandy thought. *I wish she hadn't asked. Now I have no choice.*

"I'll be here, Mrs. Benjamin," she said, letting herself out quietly.

IN THE BUSHES by the open window, Jamie smiled to himself.

CHAPTER SEVEN

Daurid Bentley was thankful that Chief Torrey—Chief Becker Torrey—was the better squash player, even though Torrey was giving away about twenty years and at least as many pounds. While David didn't believe for a minute that Torrey would ever hold losses on the squash court against him, he was just as happy that the temptation had never arisen. On an average of three times a week over the past six years, he and Torrey had played four-of-seven series, and on an average of two and a half times a week Torrey had won. It wasn't just on brains either, David had to admit. For a big, heavy man, Torrey moved like a panther—a black panther, in his particular case—and he was seemingly tireless, winning late more often than early.

They were sitting in the small, functional lounge above the courts of the Downtown Racquet Club, sipping Miller Lites from the bottle and feigning lack of interest in the two incredibly sensual young women working up lovely sweats in the court David and Torrey had vacated minutes before.

"David," Torrey said, drawing lightly on his first postgame cigarette, testing to see if his lungs were quite ready to handle it, "do you think we can rule out foul play?"

The chief had made the Reverend Morley matter David's case: That's how he preferred to operate. That's what David's father, his predecessor, had always done: unless the complications proved to be too much for one investigator, the officer who started a case remained in charge of it until it was closed or until the law of diminishing returns took over. Under both Bentley and Torrey, the twenty-four-man, thirteen-woman Jericho police force had been a model for the nation, and their morale had never flagged.

David shrugged. "I doubt it, Beck. Morley was kind of a crazy old coot by all accounts, always losing things, and sometimes he'd even forget how to get home. Pedersen says he once found the old man wandering around the middle of town at two in the morning and took him home in the cruiser. He was over eighty, Beck, and while he was apparently bright and okay most of the time, he had these lapses."

David sensed that he didn't have Torrey's undivided attention, and when he looked back down to the court, he could understand why. One of the women, the taller, darker one, was sliding her fingers under her tight white velour shorts, pulling the material away from her thighs, adjusting them for comfort. "Nice," David said softly. *Erotic as hell*, he thought.

"Um-hmm," Torrey agreed. Then, "So you think that he lost his glasses in the clearing and wandered off blind and fell into the quarry, do you?"

"Seems the most likely explanation," David said, sloshing the beer around absently and taking one last pull off the bottle. "The glasses were thick, very strong. He had to be almost blind without them."

Torrey nodded. "So the hole is out?"

"I think so. As I told you—and I'll put all the details in my written report later in the week—he apparently almost did fall down the hole. Or somebody did recently, because there were marks going down about twenty inches on one side that were probably made by shoe heels. But they stopped at an exposed tree root, and there was no evidence that he fell any further. And I did go down there." He shivered at the memory, and he knew that Torrey had seen him shake and was probably analyzing it at that very moment. No nervous movement was certainly ever lost on a good cop, not on David himself and not on Torrey.

"We've been dragging the quarry pond all day," David continued, doing his damnedest to push the hole out of the conversation. "It's useless, I think, but I don't have to tell you it's important that we at least go through the motions, so the commission and the council and the media can't say we left anything out." He drained the last of his beer and shrugged. "To be honest, Beck, I think this one is a long-goner."

Torrey raised his hand for two more beers and lit another Marlboro. "You will drag again tomorrow, though," he asked.

"Might as well," David replied. "The boat's still there. Unless you think I should try to find some other leads."

Torrey shook his head. "I don't know why," he said, "but it reminds me of a case your dad put me in charge of about twenty-odd years ago. A boy named Danny Trowbridge. Do you remember?"

"Not all that well," David admitted. "But it's funny, I was just thinking about Danny yesterday. I knew him some. We were in the same grade. And I seem to remember you and dad in our kitchen, talking about it late one night. I wasn't supposed to, but I always tried to listen when dad had cops in the house, talking about investigations. It was exciting, better than television." It was, too. Even if he hadn't left university, even if he had gone on to get a law degree, he would have been some kind of cop, somewhere.

Torrey was starting again, but not at the women below. He had that look that David knew so well, the look of a man resurrecting and reconstructing a long-past event.

"I never believed," he began, speaking slowly and

choosing his words carefully, "that Danny ended up in that pond. I know that was the reasonable conclusion, and that's what went on the final report, but I never believed it. But it came to a point where we had to let it go, and that's what we did." He grunted as he shifted his weight in the captain's chair, acknowledging that he could get as stiff as any other man from a strenuous workout.

"So what do you think happened?" David asked.

"I can't answer that. I only know what I think didn't happen."

This was, David thought, as good a time as any to try to get out what had been eating at him most of the day. "When you were working on it, was there… was there anybody who said anything about the… uh… oh, never mind, Beck."

"About the Whatelys?" Torrey asked.

"Yes." David's voice sounded very small, and he was now far less than sure that he really wanted to get into this.

"There were about half a dozen calls to the station," Torrey recalled. "I took three or four of them myself—older people, who either remembered Old Man Whately and the rest or at least said they did. One old woman insisted that long after the fire, long after the Whatelys disappeared back in 1910 or '11, she saw the old man in that clearing. Not only that, but he was dancing with the devil. That's right. That's what she said. 'Dancing with the devil.' She said there were demons there too. They were chanting, she said, words she didn't know in a language she didn't know."

"And?"

"She said there was a curse on Whately's Copse. But then, every kid who ever grew up in Jericho knows about that, don't they?" Torrey smiled. "Or was it the bogeyman's place when you were young?"

"You don't believe any of *that*, do you?" *Please say no,* David pleaded silently. Because he was afraid that he did—at least a little bit.

"I'm not a superstitious man, David," Torrey said almost gravely, "and I certainly wouldn't ever draw conclusions without basing them on the facts at hand. But who knows? There are facts and there are facts. My great grandmother was an Obeah woman, David—did I ever tell you about her? —and she knew things and she did things that I cannot explain to this day. She knew When people were going to die, even people hundreds of miles away, and she know when babies would be born—not just the month or week, but the day and hour, and what sex they would be. And she had curses, David, curses that made people well. Other things too, things that were not so nice.

"So in answer to your question, David, I just don't know. I put it all out of my mind twenty years ago, as fast as I could, and I didn't think about it again until Sunday. And," his voice changed and a smile replaced the deep concentration, "if you mention this conversation to anybody you'll be pounding a beat from midnight till dawn in perpetuity. Come on, let's get a shower."

David took one last look at the stunning women in the court below, signed the bar chit, and followed his boss down the stairs. The only reason he'd led Torrey into the conversation about Whately's Copse was to get some kind of reassurance. He hadn't counted on it resulting in the opposite effect.

"The snakes aren't very hungry tonight," Teddy said, his eyes, like Jamie's, focused intently on the activity in the terrarium.

It was true; the two grass snakes were oblivious to the bugs that Jamie was dropping one by one into the large glass case. On the other hand the three toads more than made up for the snake's lack of appetite.

"Snakes don't eat often," Jamie explained without looking away from the toad feast. "We took that in school. I told you."

"So are you going to tell me about her?" The button eyes were almost expressionless in the eerie light of the terrarium, the only light in the Benjamin basement at that moment.

"Who?" Jamie asked innocently, pretending a rapt attention to his pets' eating habits.

"Don't play games with me, boy!" Teddy snarled. "You know darn well who I mean. The babysitter. Sandy."

"She was okay, I guess." He refused to look at Teddy, but he could feel the rising impatience.

"Nice tits, I'll bet."

Jamie flushed. For some reason he wasn't sure of, he did not want to discuss Sandy with Teddy. He wanted to think about Sandy by himself, to keep her for himself. Teddy always wanted to know everything about everything, especially about girls and women. And he made everything sexy and dirty; with Miss Livingstone of Abergail or sometimes even Barbara, it didn't matter very much, but with Sandy it did. Sandy was just not the same. Sandy liked him. She'd smiled and held his hand for a long time. Jamie looked down at that hand and wished to himself that he'd remembered not to pick up all those filthy bugs with it. He should have used the other one or worn gloves or something.

"I didn't look at her ti—I didn't look there."

"Sure you did."

"She had nice eyes, Teddy," Jamie enthused, counting on his friend to get caught up in the enthusiasm as well. "They're green, almost as green as the grass. And in one there's like a little brown wedge that goes from the white to the black part—the pupil. And she has a nice nose; it turns up a little on the end. And her hair is dark brown and curly and shiny, and—"

"Does she have big tits or little tits? Are they like Barbara's or Miss Livingstone's? What are they like, Jamie?

And don't tell me you didn't look at them, because I won't believe you." It was an order. There was no mistaking that.

"How can I tell you what I don't know?" Jamie pleaded.

"You're talking too loud."

"Sorry," he whispered. They both looked toward the closed basement door, half-expecting it to be opened. Jamie sort of wished that it would and that Tom or Barbara would be standing there, ordering him upstairs. Teddy was getting more and more demanding lately, and his mind never got off of sex. Even when Jamie wanted to talk about his friends in the woods, in whom Teddy had once shown great interest, Teddy always steered the conversation back to tits and cunts (Jamie hated *that* word so much he was embarrassed to even think it, and he couldn't say it; he was pretty sure he had said it, though, the time when he really blew up at Barbara, when he was what she called "berserk" to Dr. Applebaum).

Let it go, Teddy. Please let it go.

"I'm waiting, Jamie."

He'd have to make it up. He'd have to lie,

"You know the girl in *Playboy* I showed you the other day," he began, speaking quickly, "the one in the centerfold who liked Jamaican beef patties and sensitive men and who wanted to be an ambassador some day, well Sandy's breasts are something like—"

"Tits," Teddy corrected.

"Sandy's... uh... tits are something like hers." *There, goddamn it!* Jamie screwed the lid back on the jar and lifted the terrarium roof back into place.

"I bet she has a nice pussy too, eh, Jamie?"

"Probably," Jamie sighed. "Come on, we have to go upstairs now."

CHAPTER EIGHT

"IN THE VERY DARK night of the soul," Sandy muttered to herself, "it's always three o'clock in the morning." Or was just "dark night" or maybe "darkest night?" What did it matter, anyway? In a few seconds it would be 3:01 A.M.

"Uhh?" asked the man-sized lump in the bed beside her.

"Nothing, Allan. Go back to sleep." She stroked his back gently, and in a few seconds the sleeping-person's even breathing resumed.

She wished the morning would come. And she wished that it wouldn't. Yesterday had been just about as much as her mind could handle, and if there was any truth at all to Barbara Benjamin's incredible confession, today would be worse. And tomorrow worse again. She hadn't talked about her worries with Allan. Somehow it hadn't seemed right; it would have been like betraying a trust. Barbara hadn't sworn her to secrecy, but she felt sworn anyway. When they were making love—when was it, six-and-a-half hours ago? —Allan had sensed her detachment and had asked her what was wrong, but she had told him it was nothing for him to worry his pretty little head about and flashed a convincing smile. A few minutes later she'd faked a mild orgasm, which made her feel instantly guilty and a little cheap, and this hadn't helped her overall mood one little bit.

Then Allan had fallen asleep almost immediately, as he nearly always did when they made love, even when they did it in the morning, and she had lain awake, staring at the flickering shadows on the ceiling.

For Christ's sake Sandy, get yourself together. He's only a little boy. You've looked after little boys before, some of them were hardly angels. Remember the Brenner kid, the one that ran away from home every day and you had to find him? And what about whatsisname, the one who shit the bed every night?

Yeah, but there's so much I don't know about this one.

Exactly. You don't know.

But his mother...

Look, you thought she was weird right from the beginning, didn't you? You didn't feel really comfortable, did you? And the father, he was... uh... what? Maybe there's nothing really wrong with the kid. Maybe it's the parents. Maybe when they're gone, he'll be just fine.

Maybe.

You liked the kid, didn't you?

Yes, I did.

So?

So I don't know, that's all.

I thought you wanted to be a psychologist some day. A fine psychologist you'd make: one patient'd start screaming or drooling or get violent and you'd be running out of the room. Are you really sure, like you keep saying that you're not in psych to try to come to terms with your own emotional problems, your mood swings, your yo-yoing? Come on, O'Reilly, you're twenty-four years old and you're supposed to be all grown up, so why don't you start acting like it?

I know. I will. I'll try.

Hours and hours of the same questions and answers, reworked and embroidered, but basically the same questions

and answers. The next time she looked at the clock it was
4:25 A.M. and the sky outside the open window was beginning to lighten.

JAMIE, as usual, woke with his rigid penis in his hand. He
wondered what—or who—he'd been dreaming about, and he
wished again that he could remember his dreams. But he
never could, even after Dr. Kelso had tried for so long to
teach him how.

"We can tell a lot about people's problems from their
dreams," Dr. Kelso had said. "In fact, Jamie, lots of times it's
better to know what people dream at night than what they
think in the daytime. What happens in a dream isn't real,
Jamie, but it tells us something. So you try to remember your
dreams—write them down, if you can—and we'll try to
figure out what they are saying to us."

Jamie said he didn't dream, but Dr. Kelso had explained
that everybody dreams, that if you say you don't dream, you
are just not remembering them. Jamie believed that, at least
the first part about everybody dreaming, and he tried very
hard to remember his dreams. But he just couldn't. Dr. Kelso
had said that if it didn't work after a few weeks, he would
hypnotize Jamie—if that was all right with him and his
parents and had explained hypnosis to Jamie. Jamie had been
looking forward to it, and then, before anything could
happen, Tom came home one day and said they were moving
again.

"Miss Livingstone, I presume," Teddy said, his button eyes
directed at Jamie's groin. There was a smirk on his face and a
smirk in his voice.

Jamie pulled his hand away quickly. His cheeks and ears
began to burn, "I… uh… don't know, Teddy. I never know."

"Had to be," Teddy replied. "Or maybe it was your new

friend. Sandy. Was that it, Jamie? Did you dream you were putting your thing in Sandy's cunt?"

"Noooo!" Jamie rolled out of the bed and away from the bear, propped there on the pillow, looking more and more self-satisfied. "Please, Teddy, please don't!"

"What's the matter, Jamie, is she ugly? You told me she was beautiful, Jamie. You said she had tits like the girls in the magazine. You said she had a nice pussy, too—"

"No! No, I never said that. I never saw—"

"So you were lying. Were you lying about what we were going to do with Miss Livingstone too? Is that it? We haven't talked about it for a while now, Jamie. Did you think I'd forget? You know I never forget."

Oh that. Jamie had been excited by the plan at first, but he'd had second thoughts; he couldn't see any more how it could work, and he'd begun to hope that Teddy would forget about it. There was no point in arguing with Teddy. Teddy never listened to reason. Never. When Teddy really wanted something, he really wanted it. It had been Teddy's idea to cut that picture out of the book and send it to Miss Livingstone with her head glued to it. Jamie had said that she'd know who'd done it, but Teddy wouldn't budge. He didn't care. Why should he care? Nobody was going to blame him, nobody was going to believe that anything was a stuffed bear's fault.

"Tonight," Teddy interrupted. "Let's do it tonight."

No, Jamie thought, *not tonight. Tonight Sandy will be here. She shouldn't have to be alone her first night here.* "Later on," he said. "Next week, maybe."

"Oh, sure," Teddy replied, the words dripping with sarcasm. "And next week you'll say the week after, or the week after that, and by that time we'll be moving to Seattle. Tom and Barbara will come back next week and they'll say they've found this new house and we'll be gone." He was beginning to sound less derisive and more desperate. "You've got to do it for me, Jamie. You promised."

Jamie, feeling safer, climbed back up onto the bed and turned Teddy slightly so that they were eye-to-eye. He stroked the bear soothingly. "Okay," he said softly, "we'll do it. We'll do it Friday."

Teddy seemed to stiffen.

"Friday's better," Jamie continued, speaking with more urgency. "There's a party and dance at the school, and Abergail will be there and Miss Livingstone will be alone. And I'll tell Sandy I'm going to the party, so why doesn't she go out too. It'll be easier on Friday, it'll be better."

"Well, okay," Teddy said, quite conciliatory now, "but you better keep your promise. Cross your heart and hope to die?" Jamie drew a line from his neck to his belly button, then intersected it with another line from his left nipple to the right. He did so with the proper solemnity.

Jamie had to pee, suddenly and urgently, but he didn't want to tell Teddy. He didn't feel like listening to whatever filthy remark Teddy would make about it this time.

"I'll be late for school" he said. Jamie pulled on his tattered terrycloth bathrobe and crossed the big oval braided carpet toward the door. "I got to brush my teeth."

As he closed the bedroom door behind him he heard Teddy whisper, "If you shake it more than three times, you're playing with it. Ha ha."

THE SLAMMING door saved her life. She'd been falling, siding, tumbling down a long, black tunnel, faster and faster, and there was someone, something she could not see, right behind her. She could hear its terrible rasping breathing; she could feel the unspeakable evil of it.

"Sandy?"

What? Oh, it's Jamie. Her heart was still pounding, and her eyes still unfocussed, and she lurched up from the couch not knowing whether or not her legs would support her. Jamie seemed faraway still, a dark figure against a muted-light field.

"Are you okay?" the figure asked, taking on more form and definition.

"Yeah, sure." Still in her own personal twilight zone but surfacing rapidly, she turned away briefly to tuck her T-shirt back into her jeans and snap the metal tabs together. Finally, with undisguised embarrassment, she fumbled out her apologies. "I'm sorry, Jamie. It's noon, isn't it? I'm sorry. After your mom and dad left, I just sort of... fell asleep. I didn't sleep very much last night. I'm sorry."

Jamie didn't move and he didn't speak and there was a look on his face that she couldn't quite analyze. She thought she knew, but she also thought she shouldn't jump to any hasty conclusions. If she turned out to be right, it wouldn't be all that hard to deal with. If she wasn't exactly an expert in these matters, she wasn't exactly a novice either, in fact, if her intuition was correct, the week or ten days would probably go by a lot more easily. *Little boys are such wondrous creatures,* she thought.

"I'm sorry you didn't sleep well," Jamie said, watching intently as she struggled into her sandals. Then in the same tone, he added, "Everything Barbara says about me isn't always true, you know."

She stared. *How did he know? Had he been listening? And how did he make the connection between what his mother said and the fact that I couldn't sleep?* Could he read her mind? No, nonsense! Still, she felt the undeniable need to sit for a minute; there didn't seem to be enough blood in her head; she was dizzy, and the figure in the doorway was slipping in and out of focus. Then it was beside her, sitting, touching her lightly on the arm, and she could make out the look of concern on his face.

"It's okay, Sandy," he said in a voice that she did not associate with him, a deeper voice, but not to her mind an unkind one. *Well*, she thought, *he is almost a teenager.*

"Why don't you just sit here a while?" the voice said.

He sounds so mature! She glanced down, almost nervously, to make sure it was a twelve-year-old blond boy at her side.

"I can make my own lunch." It was Jamie's voice again. Maybe she had imagined the mature voice; maybe she was still not quite awake. Her eyes stung and she could taste tinny bile in her mouth.

"I often make my own lunch," Jamie smiled brightly, bounding off the couch after one last loving, concerned pat. "I'll make you some lunch too. Is a peanut butter sandwich all right?"

She could have hugged him. Whatever his mother thought he was, whatever he might otherwise be, he was still a little boy—a beautiful little boy—who ate peanut butter sandwiches like every other beautiful little boy. Wondrous creatures. "I'll tell you what," she said, "you make the peanut butter sandwiches and I'll make lemonade. No, I'll really go all out; I'll make *limeade.* You probably can't tell just by looking at me, but my limeade has won prizes at state fairs all over America."

He laughed. They laughed together.

You're wrong about your son, Mrs. Benjamin; there's nothing wrong with him that tender loving care won't fix.

CHAPTER NINE

THAT NIGHT—WEDNESDAY—THEY sat in the dark and watched a three-hour version of *Dracula* on PBS. Louis Jordan was in it, and they agreed that he was very good in the part. Sandy had made popcorn and some more of her famous limeade, and they had tossed cushions on the floor and lain on their stomachs, side by side, until Van Helsing's final triumph. A couple of times, in the really scary parts, Jamie had reached over and taken her hand, and she had very deliberately allowed him to do so. The second time she even squeezed back, letting him know that his touch was not unwelcome and that she considered touching a nice thing for friends to do.

"What did you think?" she asked when the show was over.

"It was great," he said. Then, "My mother wouldn't have let me watch it."

"But you said…"

"I know. I lied. But it was just a little lie, Sandy, and I really did want to see it… My mother—Barbara—says I shouldn't watch things like that. She says I already have too much imagination. She says I don't need any new ideas in my head about monsters."

Sandy wasn't quite sure how to respond to that, so she didn't. Instead she gathered up the glasses and the popcorn bowl and took them to the kitchen. She bought a little more thinking time by washing the dishes immediately—bypassing the dishwasher, which she found just a bit too bourgeois for her student tastes anyway—and putting them away. When she returned to the living room Jamie was where she'd left him, but on his back, hands behind his head, eyes closed.

"You must be tired," she said. "It is after eleven and tomorrow's a school day, after all. I'm sorry I kept you up."

"Oh no, I really wanted to," he said, opening his eyes wide to prove that he was indeed fully awake and, if need be, ready to watch another movie. "I'm not tired. Honest!"

She could order him to bed, but it was better if she could make it fun. "Jamie," she began, kneeling down beside him and gently pushing his hair back off his forehead, "I think I'm in enough trouble already here. I fell asleep on the couch, I didn't make your lunch for you, and I've kept you up half the night watching horror movies…"

He began to respond but she put a finger to his lips and made a silent *shhh* with her own.

"Do you realize," she continued, "that those are all grounds for dismissal, that I could get kicked out of the babysit… the… uh… housekeeper's union?

"I'll never tell," he said, his face all serious. Then he caught her smile and went back to reassess what she had said, and he giggled. "We'll make it a secret," he said brightly. "It'll be our secret, won't it Sandy?"

"Yes," she said. "Our secret."

"I have other secrets," he informed her, his eyes flitting around the room as if he believed that somehow Barbara and Tom would suddenly and magically appear and ruin everything. "Can I tell you some of my other secrets?"

"Not now, Jamie. Now you have to go to bed and so do I.

Two hours sleep just ain't enough for a growing girl." She watched the disappointment form in his face and tried to head it off as best she could. "Tell you what, Jamie: we're going to be together for a week or longer, and I think we're going to be good friends. I think maybe we are already good friends. Anyway, we'll have lots of time for secrets. You can tell me some of yours, and I'll tell you some of mine. Is it a deal?"

"Sure. When?"

"Tomorrow. The next day. The day after that…"

"Do you have a boyfriend?" There was no reason for a simple question like that to throw her, so why did it happen that way? Why did she feel that she shouldn't answer the boy truthfully?

"Come on, Jamie, you're stalling. I've been in this business long enough to know when a kid is stalling."

"I'm not stalling," he said, standing his ground, his expression steady. "You said we'd tell each other secrets. Is your boyfriend…" He paused, and she could see that he was also trying to find the right words, that he was actually afraid of offending her.

"I go out with a guy," she said quickly, easing Jamie's unnecessary pain. "I don't know whether you'd call him a boyfriend or not. Where I grew up in Madison, we really didn't have boyfriends and girlfriends. We had friends, and some were male and some female. I go out with a guy named Allan." *There!*

"Do you love him?"

Sandy, you had better do something about this conversation before you get in too deep. But how? Have to be careful now, because I'm getting somewhere with this kid, this kid nobody is supposed to like. How do I say it?

"I like him, Jamie. But I don't love him. Like I said, we're friends."

"And you and me, we're friends too, aren't we, Sandy?"

"You bet we are, Jamie." Then, more slowly and thoughtfully, she added, "Yes, we *are* friends."

"Great!" He hugged her and ran off upstairs before she even got a chance to hug him back.

🧸

DAVID WAS DEEPLY INVOLVED in the intricate process of creating an art object, his only material a set of six swizzle sticks (three of them red) and his only equipment a glassed candle, its life almost spent, on the bar in front of him. Every so often, David treated himself to an evening of pleasant inebriation, and he refused, at least consciously, to provide an excuse for it.

"Did you ever think of enrolling in art school?" the sort-of-familiar voice asked into his right ear.

Normally he would have jumped a little and fumbled for words, but after six vodka-and tonics, spaced over maybe two hours, he had no sense of surprise and the words were ready to roll mellifluously off his tongue.

"Why, Margaret Livingstone! Unless my memory eludes me, which is far from impossible, then it is incumbent upon me to inquire as to what a nice girl like you is doing in a place like this? Or perhaps you find my approach too direct? If so, let me beg forgiveness. I am your mercy, my dear Margaret. Do with me what you will. Innkeeper, a drink for my friend. And," he regarded his glass suspiciously, "another for myself. You've arrived just in time, Margaret. I was down on my last swizzle stick. Do have a tall drink, won't you."

"I'll have what he's having," Margaret informed the bartender directly. "Polish vodka if you stock it."

"You're still the only person I ever met who orders Polish vodka, Margaret," David said. Then, "Listen, are you in a hurry or anything? Do you want to talk a little?" She eyed him warily in the mirror, and the hesitancy in her expression was not lost on him. "No," he said quickly, "no, I don't want to talk about 'us,' if that's what you're worried about. That's over." Maybe it was the soul-anesthetizing qualities of the liquor, but at that moment, however fleeting it might turn out to be, that was just about the way he felt. Just about.

It hadn't been a long affair, less than a year, but it had been what the Hollywood gossip columnist used to describe as "torrid." Then Abergail—through no fault of her own, David realized—had come between them. Four years ago she had been visiting Margaret from Indianapolis when the fire made her an orphan. Her Aunt Margaret, having lost her only sister, had kept Abergail with her. And their affair, in fact all of Margaret's affairs, so far as David knew, had died with fire as well.

"How's the girl?" he asked. He felt suddenly sober, which was not exactly welcome relief.

"Growing up. Becoming more interesting. Becoming a woman." She stirred her drink, licked the swizzle stick, and handed it over to David for his now-forgotten project. "I'm glad I did what I did, David. She needed me very badly; she needed first call on me and my time. That should begin to change soon, when she gets a little older and finds herself a young man."

"She hasn't yet?"

"No. She insists she doesn't like boys."

Oh, he thought, reaching for her cigarettes. He held the Camel awkwardly, in the manner of a person who never really learned to smoke, and accepted a light from her old Zippo lighter. He puffed half-heartedly, not inhaling, realizing how ridiculous he must look to her and anybody else who happened to be watching.

"What," he asked carefully, "will that mean for you, you know, when the kid is more on her own? Will you... uh... start dating again?"

"Haven't you heard?" she replied with exaggerated sweetness. "I've become a dyke."

"But... uh, but... I..." The cigarette had fallen out of his mouth and was somewhere in his lap, and he was brushing at it frantically. At the same time he was trying to read the expression on her face; he hoped it was a smile, preferably accompanied by a wink. Which was what he got.

"You mean you haven't heard, David? Why, I'm disappointed in you, what with you being a crack investigator and all. It's been the talk of the town for some time or at least the whisper of the town. No, I won't make you ask. It's not true; I still like men, or I think I do; I still fantasize about them, anyway. No, I'm not gay, David. I'm just an abstainer. Haven't you heard? It's all the rage in New York now. They're writing books about it. In fact, if you like I'll even sign one out for you."

David realized that for the past minute or so he hadn't exhaled, so he did so, audibly. Yes, he had heard the tumors, and no, he hadn't believed a word of them. But for a little while there she'd had him going. He ordered two more drinks, stipulating Polish vodka in both.

The alcohol was taking him over, and he had the powerful but controllable urge to reach over and pull the pins that held that golden hair in its bun and to remove the stylish but prim glasses and to open a couple more buttons of the blouse. Sometimes, when she'd come to his place directly from the library, their lovemaking had begun that way, and he had found it very, very erotic. So, remembered with a tingling in his stomach, had she.

"Margaret," he felt clumsy and stupid saying this, "when Abergail's older, and when you... uh...feel comfortable with the idea, well, you... uh...still have my phone number. And you know I still live in the same place. In fact, I think there might even be a half-bottle or so of Polish vodka around somewhere. I—"

"David," she said softly, "I promise you'll be the first to know." The bartender was at the cash register, making closing-time noises with the keys and glancing around impatiently at the five or six remaining customers scattered around the small room.

Margaret fetched her bag from the floor beside her and made a going-to-the bathroom move. "If you want to wait a few minutes," she said over her shoulder, "I'll drop you off." Then, almost as an afterthought, she said, "I assume you're not driving, not after eight swizzle sticks. That would be conduct unbecoming an officer, wouldn't it?"

Yes, it would. On the way to the men's room he dropped a dime into the pay phone and left a message with Annie, the dispatcher, telling Pedersen not to bother picking him up, that he had a ride. And were there any messages on the Morley business or otherwise? One lead maybe, Annie had said, but it could wait for tomorrow. Good. He was standing at the main entrance to the bar when Margaret emerged from the lady's john. *God*, he thought, *how I'd like to—*

"Aren't you going to save your sculpture?" she asked brightly, brushing close-by as he held the inner door open for her. "It could be worth millions someday."

The spell was broken, or at least cracked, which was probably just as well. "Nah," he answered, "those things never sell until you're dead, anyway."

THEY DROVE in silence for a while. Finally Margaret asked about the Morley case. She'd read about it in the newspaper and knew that he was in charge. He sketched in for her what he knew, which was little more than she'd already read. The business of the strange hole he purposely omitted, however. When he was finished with the telling, an idea flashed across his mind.

"Margaret," he said, turning to face her profile, "is there much material in the library on the early history of Jericho? I mean, say from about 1875 or so on?"

"Yes, there is. It's quite extensive. My predecessor, Mrs. Vogel, fancied herself an amateur historian, and she collected and wrote a great deal about the town. Is there anything specific you have in mind?"

"Yes," he said. "It relates indirectly—maybe—to the case. I'm really interested in anything that has anything to do with Whately's Copse and the Whately family in general."

"I'll check it out tomorrow," she promised. "Look, we're home—at least you are."

With undisguizable reluctance he undid the seat belt and reached for the door handle.

"I don't suppose," he said, trying to make what he wanted to ask easy to gracefully refuse, "that I could talk you into a Polish vodka-and-tonic for the road, could I?"

"You men are all alike," she laughed. Then was serious. "No, David. Not now. Not yet."

"Give my best to Abergail," he said, meaning it. "And if you get that stuff for me, would you call me at the station? If I'm not there, you can leave a message." He closed the car door quietly, respecting the late hour. "Good night, Margaret. It was good seeing you again."

"Good night, David. Yes, yes it was."

He watched the car ease out, and he followed it with his eyes until the headlights disappeared around the corner six blocks away.

CHAPTER TEN

"SANDY and I had fun tonight, Teddy. We watched *Dracula* on TV and we ate popcorn and we talked and you know something else, Teddy? We held hands. I think she likes me, Teddy."

"Hmmph," the bear replied, sourly.

But Jamie was excited and thus oblivious to his friend's foul mood. "She does like me, Teddy, I know she does. And she really is beautiful, too. She says we're friends, Teddy… Teddy, what's the matter?"

"Big deal," Teddy mumbled.

"What?"

"I said, big deal. What's the matter with you, you deaf?"

"Don't you want me to have friends?" Jamie asked, hurt and confusion intermingled in his voice.

"You have me," Teddy said, his tone icy. "We're friends. Or at least we once were. What is it, Jamie, do you think you're getting too old for me, like Tom and Barbara said? Is it time for Old Teddy to get lost?"

Jamie felt the tears welling in his eyes and the lump forming in his chest. Immediately he abandoned what he was doing—buttoning his pajama top—and took Teddy gently into his arms. He caressed the bear along the zipper on the back, the way Teddy always liked it; and he promised in a quavering voice his undying friendship.

Teddy, after maintaining a long silence, finally spoke. "You're not my first kid, Jamie, and…" he sighed, "I guess now you won't be my last. But seven years is a long time, Jamie, it's more than half as long as you've been alive. I thought… I thought we needed one another, but I guess I was wrong. Oh well."

Jamie had never seen Teddy this way before, and his little boy's mind was having trouble handling it. Teddy had always been so strong, always knowing what to do. Now he sounded so tired, so hurt. The tears ran down Jamie's face now and got lost in the flannel fur of Teddy's shoulder.

"Teddy! Teddy!" he wept. "It'll be okay. Honest it will. Nothing's going to happen to us. I won't let it!"

"But you're going to tell her secrets," Teddy sniffled. "You're going to tell her our secrets. You're going to spoil everything, Jamie."

"No, Teddy. I won't tell her anything you don't want me to tell her." He held the bear at arm's length, but still lovingly, so that Teddy could look into his eyes and know that he was not lying. "I won't do anything you don't want me to do."

"Cross your heart," Teddy ordered.

"And hope to die," Jamie obeyed.

Teddy managed a crooked smile. "Now tell me about the Dracula movie. Especially about Renfield."

Jamie gasped. How did Teddy know about Renfield, the rat-man, the one who caught flies and fed them to spiders and then ate the spiders? How did he know?

"I know a lot of things, Jamie," Teddy said, answering the unspoken thought, the unasked question. "A lot of things."

AFTER ANOTHER BAD START, Sandy had slept well and deeply. The alarm, as always, set her heart a-racing, and with eyes still closed she reached out for it. *Shit. Wrong side.* Her own night table was on the left. But here in this strange bedroom the night table and alarm clock were on the right. She rolled over toward it, then froze. Her eyes were open now. Wide.

"Jesus Christ, Jamie!"

He just sat there on the cedar chest at the foot of the bed. She had started him, but the odd little smile he'd been smiling was still frozen on his face. She saw immediately where he was looking and at the way the nightie fell open, uncovering an errant breast. Then, just to make sure, she yanked the covers up to her throat and held there with her left hand while fumbling for the now-dying alarm clock with her right. All she managed to do was knock it to the floor, where it mercifully breathed its last.

"Jesus Christ, Jamie!" She repeated, almost as if she was expressing her shock for the first time. "What the hell do you think you're doing?"

Her sleeping state had abruptly ended, but consciousness had not yet fully taken over. About all she could understand was that Jamie's surprise at her outburst had been almost as great as hers at his presence in the room. He looked terrified now, on his feet and backing away, his hand at his mouth, patting absently at trembling lips.

"I… uh… um… I…" he stammered, his eyes blinking and huge. "I… I wasn't doing anything honest I wasn't!" He backed into a chair and, unable to keep his balance, fell back into it with a *whoomph.*

She could not hold back the laughter. It was like something out of a movie; a W. C. Fields or a Marx Brothers movie. The spell had been broken, the shock and anger dissipated. And the more she looked at him sitting there, his face, uncomprehending, but losing its fear, the harder she laughed. Finally, when Jamie was really sure that it was all right, he laughed too. Then silence, as they wiped away the tears and regarded one another across the room.

"What you did wasn't funny," Sandy said finally, her voice not quite as grave as she'd been striving for. "I mean you coming into the room and watching me. You can't do that Jamie. That's not right, not acceptable." The proper gravity was there now; she didn't have to fake it. "Didn't your mother or father ever teach you about respecting other people's privacy?"

"I wasn't doing anything," he replied in a whisper, his eyes flicking nervously toward the door, as if planning a running escape. "I was just looking, just watching you sleep." He leaned forward, his face flushed and looking very earnest. "You look great when you're asleep, Sandy. Really beautiful, I mean."

"Flattery will get you nowhere, young man." She saw his blank expression and realized that—and this was hard to believe—he wasn't quite sure what the cliché´ meant. Then came a stirring of comprehension. "Haven't you ever heard that before, Jamie," she asked kindly.

He shook his head. "I guess so, and I think I kind of know what it means, but I never heard it. I mean, nobody ever said it to me." Silence again.

Poor, poor Jamie, Sandy thought. She now had no indignation left for the boy, and she told herself that what he'd done really wasn't all that bad anyway. Boys will be boys. And girls will be girls; she recalled that morning at the Provincetown Inn on Cape Cod when she'd come back from playing on the breakwater and found her parents making love. They hadn't pulled the curtains together properly, and she could see the two of them quite clearly. Though she had known it was wrong to watch, she'd been fascinated, and it was only when some other people had come out of the room next door that she had moved away. She had been twelve at the time, Jamie's age.

He stood now, with his hands stuffed in his pockets twisting a little from side to side and edging toward the door. But his eyes were still on her, in fact, they had been fixed on her the whole time.

"I'm sorry, Sandy," he said, "I didn't mean to make you mad." Then, to her relief, he turned away and reached for the doorknob. When he was halfway out the door, he turned and faced her again. He seemed composed now. "I didn't do anything though," he said. "I was just watching. I wouldn't do anything to hurt you."

Then, in what seemed to her to be a very deliberate afterthought, he added, "I'm just a little boy, you know."

And he was gone.

Yes, Jamie, you're just a little boy. At least you look like a little boy. But sometimes... sometimes you don't act like a little boy at all. Sometimes your eyes... oh for Christ's sake, Sandy, get your ass out of bed and make some breakfast and stop seeing things that aren't there!

"WELL?"

"I saw her breasts, Teddy. I mean, I saw one of them."

"Tits, Jamie. Tits. And?"

"It was... it was like I said, Teddy. Just like the girl in *Playboy*. Not as big, I don't think, but the same shape. And the nipple part was smaller and it was really pink. And the other part, the part around the nipple, was pink too, not like Barbara's."

"Like Miss Livingstone's, I'll bet. Probably not as nice. What about her cunt?"

"I didn't see it, Teddy. She woke up. She caught me."

"Well, Jamie, soon you'll have to be smarter, won't you. You promised, Jamie. We made a bargain."

"I know, Teddy.

"So?"

"Tonight, Teddy. I'll try again tonight."

DAVID BENTLEY WOKE at his usual time, a quarter after seven, and was halfway out of bed before he realized that he was not a well man. In truth, he was a patently unwell man, a man afflicted with the mother and father of all hangovers. He sat on the edge of the bed, his head pounding, hating himself for any number of reasons, not the least of which being that he knew he looked like a cliché. The open Courvoisier bottle, drained but for a thimbleful, taunted him from the low dresser that also served as his nightstand. *Where the hell was the snifter? Oh yeah. On the rug. On its side, next to that dark, wet stain.*

"God," he muttered, "if you get me through the day, I swear I'll never ever do it again."

Sure, Bentley. He's heard that one before. Next time, stick with vodka all the way, and for Chrissake quite trying to play the Casablanca role, because you're not worth a shit at it.

He stumbled into the kitchen, filled the electric kettle and plugged it in, he dropped coffee beans into that grinder, wincing all the while as they landed like golf balls on a tin roof; and bracing his nerve endings against the inevitable, he pushed the button on the side. The effect was like a cement mixer—just before it explodes. Miraculously, he lived through it.

While the coffee was dripping into the Pyrex pot, he found the bathroom, where he examined his face for permanent damage while screwing up his courage for the shower, which, he was certain, would rip the skin right off him. It almost did, but right at the last minute he managed to rescue himself.

The coffee tasted like crankcase oil—boiling crankcase oil

—and his stomach came within one lurching roll of rejecting it. *I should eat something*, he told himself; but the thought brought the coffee back up into his gullet, and he decided to forgo the pleasure. The clock on the stove claimed it was now 7:49. For the first time he looked toward the window and ascertained that it was another in an immoderately long stretch of sunny summer days. Well, at least he could wear his sunglasses with a certain amount of impunity.

He dressed quickly in an all-fresh uniform—which made him feel marginally better—and strapped on the issue .357 Magnum. Unlike most of the other officers, he wore the gun butt-backward on his right hip, accessible to either hand. Although he had never killed or wounded a man with that gun, he fired it a number of times in anger, most recently at a couple of punks fleeing in a stolen LTD from a service station robbery. Shooting left-handed, while driving between ninety and ninety-five miles an hour, he had put a bullet into the LTD's trunk. The slug then passed through the backseat, between the two men in the front, through the dash and firewall, and blew the carburetor completely to pieces. The punks had climbed out with their hands on their hands, and their frightened eyes never left the black hole of a gun muzzle he kept pointed at them, until Helen McLachlan drove up and cuffed the two of them.

Automatically David checked the cylinder and then placed the hammer back on the empty chamber. He holstered the weapon, adjusted the gun belt to distribute the weight a little more comfortably, and eased out into the sunshine. After the first wave of pain assed, climbed into his prized candy-colored '67 Camaro and slipped into that morning rush-hour traffic.

Silently he blessed his father for buying a house, his house now, so close to the police station. Five minutes. *I should call dad and mom some time*, he thought, feeling guilty for his recent neglect of them. *I wonder how they're doing out there in Santa Barbara.*

David checked in at the station, keeping his sunglasses on inside. This, naturally, provoked the usual—and painfully accurate—comments on his inability to cope with alcohol. He discovered, nevertheless, that he was still officially on the Morley disappearance. A farmer named Engstrom, who lived about halfway between the town and the paper mill, had called the station last night (oh yes, now he remembered vaguely), claiming to have seen an old man who fit Morley's description walking along a side road. He hadn't been sure if it had been on Sunday or Monday, but he knew it was around dusk. He hadn't called before because he hadn't even known about Morley being missing until he'd read Wednesday's—yesterday's—paper.

"Anything else?" David asked Annie Goring, the night dispatcher, who was just going off-duty.

"Nah, not directly. Just a couple of nut calls."

"Nut calls?"

"Yeah. You know. People claiming the devil got the old man in Whately's Copse. Old people, I think. Senile, probably."

"Did you get their names?" David asked. He couldn't share the smile on Annie's face.

CHAPTER ELEVEN

Despite her hurry-up efforts in the bathroom and in dressing, Sandy arrived in the kitchen just as Jamie was dropping the last of the crispy bacon onto the pad of paper towel. Four slices of bread were in the toaster, waiting for her, and four brown, range-free eggs sat in an off-white china bowl beside the electric frying pan. The kettle had just begun to boil; there was the prescribed amount of coffee in the percolator, the table was set; and the orange juice poured. Again she had been one-upped, again the keeper found herself in the uncomfortable role of *keepee*.

"Well, Jamie," she said with just a little too much cheerfulness, "you're certainly going to make some woman a great wife some day."

Jamie again looked mystified. *Another bomb-out, O'Reilly. You're doing really well for yourself.* "All that means, Jamie," — she tried to recoup—"well… it's kind of a joke. I mean, people used to tell women who were good at cooking or sewing and things like that, that they'd make some man a good wife some day. And now, with women's liberation, we've kind of turned it around and made it into a joke, and…" *Oh shit!* "Never mind, Jamie. All I wanted to really say is that you're a wonder."

"Oh?" he said brightly. "Thank you, Sandy. Do you like your eggs fried over or sunny side up?"

"Why don't I…" *No, let him finish what he'd started, and try to catch up with lunch and dinner.* "Over," she said, "easy."

She watched as he expertly broke the eggs, one handed, against the edge of the bowl and dropped them into the crackling bacon fat; he checked his watch, waited perhaps fifteen or twenty more seconds, then dealt with the toaster.

"You are a very efficient young man," she marveled. "Where did you learn to cook like that, from your mother?"

"Some," he replied, taking the compliment with apparent equanimity. "And from my other… uh… baby sitters. There was a black lady in Atlanta who could really cook stuff—everything—and she liked teaching me. I mean, at first she did. Later she told me to stay out of the kitchen. And later, when Barbara and Tom came home, the lady left without even saying good-bye to me." He looked out the window for a moment, then went on, "Barbara says we don't have much luck with baby-sitters; she says that good help is hard to find these days." He made a worried look, and for the first time Sandy could see some of Barbara Benjamin in her son's face. Of her husband, there was not a trace.

The toaster made a pop, and the four slices of bread, now perfectly browned, rose in their slots. Jamie lifted them out quickly, using just his fingertips to avoid burns, and distributed them on two dinner plates. He buttered them there, and next, just as expertly, he flipped the eggs. In about thirty seconds he slid eggs and bacon onto the plates beside the toast and brought the plates to the table.

"Coffee?" he asked.

Jamie ate greedily, she noted; but then, so did she. As bacon-and-egg breakfast went, this was as good as she'd ever eaten. When they finished she told him so, and he shrugged happily. Then he stood and began to carry the dirty dishes toward the sink.

"Stop!" Sandy ordered. "I'm going to do those dishes if I have to tie you to a chair." This time, thank God, he understood she was joking and laughed with her.

"Sandy," he said to her back, "I want to tell you my secret now. You know, the one I promised to tell you."

"Okay, Jamie," she said. Then, checking the kitchen clock and seeing that it was 8:20, she added, "But you'd better try to make it quick; you'll have to leave for school in a few minutes."

"Oh, I've got lots of time. Anyway, about my secret: first you have to promise never to tell anybody, ever."

"I promise."

"You have to cross your heart and hope to die."

"Okay," she said, making a half-hearted swipe at crossing herself.

"No, Sandy, it's like this..." He was out of his chair and easing himself between her and the sink. He demonstrated and she tried to follow his instructions. But he still wasn't satisfied. He took her hand in his and traced the proper cross. And on the horizontal he managed to brush her breasts. She pretended not to notice but made a mental note to herself to start wearing a bra and to keep it on for the duration of the assignment. It wasn't that she was offended. She couldn't even be sure that Jamie's touch had been intentional; it just seemed to be a good idea.

"Okay, Jamie," she said. "My life is in your hands now. What's the big secret?"

He checked her face to make sure she was taking the matter seriously, and Sandy, realizing she was being scrutinized, made herself look deeply and sincerely interested.

"Well," he began, "first I have to tell you about the hole in the woods. Do you know the woods I mean, not too far from here? It's called Whately's Copse, I think, and nobody's supposed to go there. It's supposed to be dangerous. But it isn't, not really, not if you're careful and don't fall down the hole."

Sandy nodded. She had a vague idea about the woods he was talking about, but the college was five miles out of town, so that, even after four years of living in the area she did not know all the details about Jericho. But Whately's Copse sounded familiar. Oh yes, that's where they were looking for that old man, that reverend, who'd gone missing on Sunday. Her mind made a tenuous connection between what Jamie was telling her and the missing preacher but could carry it no farther than that. Besides, Jamie was talking again.

"It's not a big hole—I mean it isn't too wide across—but it's kind of deep. I might be the only person who knows about it, I mean *really* knows about it!"

"Just a minute, Jamie," Now she remembered. There was something in the paper about a hole, about a policeman had gone down into it looking for the reverend, but how he'd found nothing. "Is that the same hole I read about in the paper? If it is, then a lot of people know about it now. The paper said it was probably caused by the earthquake we had three years ago..." She could see his face getting cloudy, but she didn't interpret it properly. "I'm sorry, Jamie," she said, touching his hand across the table, where they had repaired for his secret-telling, "I interrupted you. Please continue your story."

But the cloud didn't pass. "I've got to go," he said with some urgency. "I'll be late for school. I'll tell you tonight. I promise." Then he was up and gone out the screen door.

DAVID'S INTERVIEW with Gus Engstrom, the farmer who'd called about maybe having seen Reverend Morley, was mercifully short. And 'mercifully' was the operative word, because Engstrom was spreading manure when David arrived at the farm, and the smell of fresh cow shit did nothing good for David's still churning, hangover stomach. Engstrom had taken one look at the good glossy photograph of Reverend Morley and shook his head. The picture in the paper had been taken at some church fund-raising a decade or so before. That one looked more like the man Engstrom had seen. But no, he had definitely not seen the man in David's picture, that he was sure about.

After David thanked Engstrom, he climbed back into the cruiser, and a couple of miles later, he allowed himself the luxury of breathing through his nose again. A radio call to the station told him he had no pressing business or new instructions, so he informed the day dispatcher that he would be leaving the car in about ten minutes. He gave the phone number of a Mrs. A. E. Bronwyn on Jackson Street. That's where he'd be until further notice.

To his relief, Mrs. Bronwyn was a delightful old lady with pure white, recently permed hair, rimless bifocals, and a smile that belonged to the grandmother of everybody's dreams.

They sat outside on a shaded verandah and sipped, of all things, Guinness Stout. Mrs. Bronwyn—who insisted on being called Alice—took one look at him and said he didn't look well, and diagnosed his condition immediately. Alice had insisted on treating him with her own favorite remedy, and, in fact, said she'd love to join him. The warm, heavy, bitter brew had made David gag at first, but now, half-a-bottle later, he was beginning to feel whole and human again.

"Now, Mrs. Bron—Alice—you called the station last night about Reverend Morley's disappearance. Can you tell me what you know?"

"Well, officer..." When she finished her statement, he would insist that she call him David; where were his manners, anyway? "...I know you're going to think I'm a silly old woman

—God knows, my children do; and maybe I am—and I don't want you to humor me if you think I'm a fool. And, by the way, I'm not one of those people who claims to have seen old Jared Whately dancing with the devil under the light of the full moon." David raised an eyebrow in surprise, and he saw it was not lost on her. "So you've already heard," she said, still studying his face. "I was almost certain you would, sooner or later. Oh yes, I've heard those stories and maybe they're true and maybe they aren't, but I don't know for sure, and I don't talk Out loud about things I don't know about. Reporter's training, I guess."

"Reporter?"

"Yes, that's right. When I was young, just after the Great War, I woke for the old *Advocate*. You wouldn't remember it, but your father would—I'm just assuming you're Chief Bentley's son; you're his spitting image. You are the old chief's son, aren't you?"

"Mrs. Br—Alice—you are a remarkable woman. Yes, I'm David Bentley the Third. You can call me David. When dad and mom left for California a few years ago, I dropped the 'Third.' But please go on, I'm fascinated." And he was.

Alice Bronwyn had been born Alice Smart in the year 1901, the first year of the new century—did he know that, did he know that 1900 was really the last year of the nineteenth century?—and had lived almost all of her life here in Jericho. At sixteen she had graduated from high school and gone off to Madison for a course in secretarial training. In the labor-short spring of 1918, she had easily landed a clerical job at the *Advocate*. And by the time the men started returning the following winter, she had already made herself a name as both reporter and editor. She had kept the job until 1931, when the Depression finally killed the newspaper. In a way, the economic circumstances had made her decision easier. She had been four months pregnant at the time, and her lawyer husband had been urging her to quit, despite how much her small income helped in those hard times.

Even though she had talked for nearly fifteen minutes and had not come to any point about Reverend Morley of Whately's Copse, David's interest never flagged.

I could sit here and listen to her all day, he thought, *and all night*.

She excused herself for a moment, and while she was gone, David closed his eyes and dozed lightly to the bored chirps and insect buzzes. He was feeling... well, amiable. When he opened his eyes again—he guessed it was only a few minutes later—there was a plate of sandwiches and a pitcher of iced tea on the table between them. Alice pointed, and he chose a chopped egg on whole wheat. She did the same and resumed her story.

"Not many people in Jericho ever saw the Whatelys, David. They kept to themselves. In fact, the only one I ever saw was Jared, the old man. He used to bring the milk in every morning to my father's dairy. He'd come in the dark, mostly, when the town was still asleep, but a couple of times I got up early and went down there with my dad, and I saw him. Dad called him a 'very odd duck.' Dad was English, by the way. Came over in 1892 and opened the first dairy in this area. Anyway, I saw Old Jared, and he was one of those people you don't forget. He was small and very dark, not Negro dark, more like Mediterranean or Black Irish; but the shape of his face was all wrong for that, it was kind of Swedish. You know, a long thin nose and deep-set eyes sort of close together. And those eyes, you'd think they'd be brown or even black, but they weren't; they were amber colored, almost golden, and..." David shivered suddenly, remembering the hole, what he had almost convinced himself he hadn't seen down there. He could tell that Alice had taken in that shiver, too, but she just kept talking. "...and they were small, just a bit too small for the face... Is there something the matter?"

"No, it's okay," David replied. "You just made me think of something that frightened me—when I was a kid."

His response was too quick and too feeble, and he knew she didn't believe him; but she was a gracious woman, and she let it pass. Her story went on for another hour-and-a-half, and while it was all fascinating, David's cop's mind zeroed in on and retained thoroughly a few major and possibly useful points.

First, the 1911 fire's origin had never been determined, although Alice's father, deputy chief of the volunteer fire department of the day, went to his death believing it had been set deliberately. A hunch, he had told Alice when the then-nine-year-old girl had asked, but she still believed he knew more than that.

Second, the disappearance of the Whately family was even more mysterious, more bizarre, than David had thought. The snow had been five feet deep, with drifts three times that high, and the roads, what there were of them, impassable to even the most modern of cutters. And, finally, there were no footprints found around the Whately farm except for one set leading to and from the barn and house. If the snow had filled in the others, why not the ones between the house and barn? No answer; not even a guess. Besides, it hadn't snowed that night and the wind was calm.

Third—and David had known this already—the children of Jericho were warned all their lives never to set foot in Whaley's Copse. Alice thought this had been true even before the fire, but it was one of the few things to do with the story she wasn't fully certain about. As adventurous and brave a child as she'd been, she too had staved prudently away. When other children disappeared From Jericho—and she could remember at least two before Danny Trowbridge—most parents had seized the opportunity to drill home the lesson to their own kids: see what happens when you disobey, when you go to that place? The copse had been thoroughly searched, of course, but not a trace of the lost children had been found. And that was before the quarry, which had been one of Roosevelt's New Deal work projects in the mid-Thirties, so there was no question of their drowning in that.

"Well," David said, standing up to leave, "we should have more witnesses like you."

He then thanked Alice two or three times for her generosity, from the stout to the lunch to the information she had provided, and he promised to drop around again as soon as he had a chance. On the way back to the station he stopped at Roy's Florists and ordered a dozen yellow roses, for immediate delivery "To a Great Lady."

CHAPTER TWELVE

WHEN MRS. LYNDE dismissed the class a half-hour early that June afternoon, even Jamie had joined in the applause, surprising himself as much as the other kids and Mrs. Lynde herself. What's more, he was the second kid out the door, a somewhat astounding break with personal tradition.

As soon as he was outside the building, he broke into a run, which was something else he simply never did, not even to get away from taunts and bullying. His body had been at school that day, but his mind had been elsewhere, as evidenced by the fact that, for the first time ever, he'd been knocked out of a spelling contest—or "bee" as Mrs. Lynde called it—for his failure to remember the "e's-rule" for cemetery: "E's, or *ease* into the ground." Of course the other children had cheered when he lost, but he'd been so preoccupied that he'd hardly noticed. Mrs. Lynde, however, had assigned all the offenders extra homework.

In the morning, when Sandy had mentioned the stuff in the paper about the hole, Jamie had gone into a state of near panic. Sure he knew, because he was there watching, that the hole itself was no longer a secret. The cop knew, and the rest of the searches did too. But, Jamie realized, and the rest of the searchers did too. But, Jamie realized, if it was in the paper, then others might come and learn the real secret. He had, that morning, seriously considered skipping school and going directly to the woods. But that would have got Sandy in trouble as well as himself. And then, when the lunch hour finally came, he'd thought about not going home, but then Sandy would have been worried about him. And besides, it was really good to be with her, and he had come to jealously look forward to the time they had alone together. Fortunately, she hadn't reopened the matter of the hole in the woods and he, of course, had very deliberately avoided it.

Now, at last, he was coming to the clearing. He stopped running and stood hidden by the trees and brush that grew on the periphery. He listened to satisfy himself that there were no other people around, no searchers in the woods. Then he took a few more silent steps to a point where he could see the whole clearing. It was quite empty.

"There's nothing to worry about," he assured himself for perhaps the tenth time that day.

He was at the hole's lip now, and he dropped down into his lying position, face peering down into the darkness. Everything seemed precisely the way he'd left it two days before, and there were no signs that the hole had been revisited by anybody. Some of the anxiety and tension left him, but some still remained. Who knows who came out here for a look, and who knows what they saw? A vision of schoolchildren, teenagers maybe, standing around the hole throwing in rocks came and went in Jamie's mind.

"Hello," he said tentatively. "It's Jamie again. Remember?" No response. "Hi down there," he shouted, cupping his hands to his mouth. "It's okay. I'm alone. It's safe."

The scratching sound was soft and far-off at first, but he heard it grow louder and more distinct. Yes, it was them. They were still all right! Then the other sound came, the grunting that he thought sounded more like pigs than anything else he'd ever heard, and which he had decided was their "language." He mimicked the sound as best he could, not knowing what he was saying, but hoping it was what he was thinking: "Come out. I am your friend."

He saw the first set of yellow eyes, blinking upward at him and the light. Then the second set. And the third. The unintelligible jabber in the pit grew louder and more prolonged, and Jamie was more sure than ever that his friends, troglodytes or whatever they were, were actually talking to one another. He also began to think they were talking about him. And he thought he saw, though he was uncertain because of the darkness below, one of the creatures raise a hand (*well, what else would you call it?*) and point at him.

Jamie smiled and waved. "Guess what," he said. "I'm going to tell somebody else about you. But don't worry, She won't tell. She's a really nice lady, and she's really beautiful and smart, too. I bet she'll even know what you like to eat."

The pig noises below suddenly stopped, and he saw a fourth set of eyes appear, then a fifth. The trogs were in a close group now right about where Jamie figured was the middle of the bottom of the hole. They were watching him, and what's more, they were listening. They had to be.

"I'll be back tomorrow," he said, rising to his hands and knees. "And maybe I'll try to bring her with me."

SANDY LISTENED to the story with an increasingly heady mixture of fascination and horror. With a great effort of will, she kept from interjecting and contradicting.

For the first time since she had met Jamie Benjamin, she began to appreciate just what his mother had been trying to tell her. This was no simple little childhood fantasy, this tale of Jamie's; this was awfully close to a full-blown psychosis.

For one of the few times in her young life, Sandy O'Reilly felt almost completely inadequate, her B.S. in psychology no more use to her than her high school diploma. The only thing she did know was that she could not say or do anything to crush the boy's illusion. What if she sent him over the line? That line seemed closer and thinner than she'd ever suspected before. And anyway, she had no right to interfere in this family. Next week they'd be gone from her life. No, the best thing she could do was to play along.

"What... uh... what did you say you thought the Creatures were, Jamie?" she asked, listening carefully to every word she spoke and every inflection, trying to hide her true feelings and make her interest sound genuine.

"Troglodytes," he replied. "It means cave dwellers. Sometimes they're just called trogs." If he had sensed her concern, he wasn't showing any signs of it. "After I first saw them—it was when we were on Easter break, like I told you—I went to the library and I looked through some books and I found them. I don't know if they're really troglodytes, but I think so. They're small, about the same size as me, and they've got hair all over them, and scales. And little yellow eyes, like a cat or something. And I think they have claws, and really sharp teeth."

"And they live in this hole?" *Think fast, Sandy.* "Is this... uh... the first time you've ever seen them, Jamie I mean here in Jericho? You never saw them in any of the other places you lived?"

"No," he said. "Never... Hey, do you want to come and see them? I told them you might come. I told them about you and about how I was going to tell you my secret. How about it, Sandy? We can go right now, it's a long time until dark. This is the third longest day of the year, you know."

Don't answer right away. Keep him talking. If you go there, and you don't see anything—well, of course you won't see anything, you idiot!—then what do you do, tell him he's lying, tell him he's imagining things, tell him he's crazy? If you're going to shatter this boy's fantasy, Ms. Sandra O' Reilly, you damn well better have something to replace it with.

Okay, carefully now. "Jamie, I know you told your friends about me, but maybe they didn't understand. I mean, if they are what you think, troglodytes, I'm sure they don't speak English. If I went there with you, they might not like it. They might hide from both of us. I mean, they must have hidden from the search parity, right? Maybe you're the only one they trust." *Not bad, O'Reilly, it looks like you can actually put one over on a disturbed twelve-year-old boy.*

Jamie thought about it for a while, and Sandy could almost see his mind going over and over her argument looking for flaws but unable to find any.

"Yeah," he said finally, "you're probably right." Sometimes he sounded so old, so… *wise.* And sometimes he sounded so terribly young and trusting and vulnerable. "Thank you Sandy, thank you for believing me!"

She forced a smile and nodded. But she felt like a lying shit.

"Hi, Teddy," he said quietly, closing the door behind him.

"I wondered when you'd get around to me," the bear said huffily. But the tone was lost on Jamie, who was much too excited to pick it up. He had so much to tell his friend.

"She believed me, Teddy, she really did! She asked me questions and everything, and I could tell she believed me! And she'd have come with me to see the trogs too, but she was afraid she'd scare them away or make them mad at me. Isn't that great, Teddy, isn't she great!"

"Yeah, great," Teddy's voice dripped with sarcasm. "And I suppose you told her about the old man, too, right? I bet she's on the phone right now, calling the cops."

"No, I didn't. I promised I wouldn't and I didn't. Besides, Teddy, she wouldn't tell anybody our secret. She crossed her heart."

"Jamie, Jamie! When are you going to learn that you can't trust anybody except me? You told Dr. Kelso things and Dr. Applebaum. You said it was okay, that you trusted them—well, Kelso, anyway—and then they went and blabbed to Barbara and Tom. Be careful, Jamie. Be very, very careful."

DR. GALNICOFF'S answering machine explained that he would be off enjoying a well-deserved rest in north Scotland until July 17th, and that he would appreciate it if callers did not leave their names and numbers at the sound of the beep, but simply called back after his return. There were a couple of other psych profs at the college to might be helpful, Sandy knew, but Mike Galnicoff was the only one with whom she could really feel comfortable discussing, a case as bizarre as Jamie's:

Next, she phoned Allan.

"Hi," she said in a little voice.

"Well," he replied in that slightly overblown manner he adopted when he wanted to make a show of his indignation. "I thought I'd been kissed off permanently when you shoved me out the door the other day."

"For a doctoral candidate in experimental psych you sure have a way of misreading the signs," she shot back. Then, more conciliatory, "I had things on my mind, Allan, and I didn't really want to talk about them then. I know I was bitchy. I'm sorry."

"Apology accepted," he said, "and case closed. So, how's it going down there? You and the kid getting along all right?"

Okay, Sandy, this is why you called in the first place, now what are you going to say, how are you going to phrase it? Yes, Allan, we're getting along fine, but we have this problem because he wants to introduce me to some friends of his who live in a hole out in the woods? Yes, Allan, except for the fact that he's stark, raving mad?

"Actually," she eventually said, "something's just come up that sort of worries me. I called Mike, but he's away for another three weeks. I'd really like to talk to you about it, Allan. I know child psych isn't your field, but I'd just like to kick it around with you and see what you think."

There was a short silence on the other end of the phone. Finally, he said, "Well?"

"It's too complicated on the phone, Allan. Can… can you come over?"

"If it's as serious as you're making it sound, not by what you say but by the way you're not saying it—there, now who were you accusing of misreading signs?—then I'll come," he said. "But if it can keep till the weekend, I'd appreciate it. Actually, when you called I was just packing an overnight bag. Remember I was telling you about needing to see those new chimp films? Well, I got a call from Dr. Bleir's secretary up in Madison, and I'm booked into the screening room for eight thirty A.M. tomorrow. But if it's really important, I'll cancel. I mean that, sweetheart, I'm not just fishing."

She wanted to say, "Cancel," but she just couldn't justify it. For one thing, those films were vital to Allan's nearly completed thesis. And for another, Jamie had given her no reason to be afraid of him; in fact, he'd been nothing other than loving and trusting. As she pondered her impressions of him more, she began to think that maybe she had just been overreacting. Maybe she still believed Barbara Benjamin's incredible "confession" more than she'd thought.

"No," she said, "it's not urgent. The weekend will be fine."

"Tell you what," Allan replied, with a certain amount of relief, "I should be back in town about seven or eight tomorrow night, depending on how long my meeting with Dr. Bleir lasts in the afternoon. I'll grab a bottle of good wine, and we'll talk about whatever's bothering you. And," he added, dropping his voice the way he always did when he was telegraphing his sexual desire, something she always found, for lack of a better description, cute, "if that doesn't help I know a sure cure for female neuroses."

Well, she thought, *that isn't a bad idea at all.*

"You're a disgusting man, Allan Dressen, and some day God will strike you impotent."

"Probably," he laughed. "I just hope it isn't before tomorrow night."

CHAPTER THIRTEEN

FOR THE FIRST time in days, Teddy seemed to be in a good mood. Even Jamie, who'd been having some second thoughts about the "Miss Livingstone Project," especially since Sandy's arrival, was getting excited about it once again. He was particularly pleased with himself because the "note" looked so slick and professional, as neat as anything he'd ever seen on TV. He held up the page to Teddy's approval, and the little button eyes seemed to dance.

"Only a few more words, Teddy," Jamie said, putting down the page and flipping through *Newsweek* for an "instructed" and a "harm." He already had the other words put aside, and the pasted-down note would ultimately end with: "If you do as instructed, she will come to no harm."

Jamie found what he was looking for on page 37, in a two-column story about the President ordering the State Department to look into some dumb crisis in the Far East. He laid his steel-edged ruler above and below the words and cut precisely with the X-acto knife. Using the sharp point, he lifted the words off the magazine page and onto the narrow ribbon of glue he'd spread on the note. He filled in the final sentence, put down the knife, started to remove the rubber gloves he'd borrowed from the kitchen.

"No," Teddy cautioned. "Put it in the envelope first. No fingerprints, remember. They can take prints off anything."

Jamie complied. The envelope was already addressed with "miss" and "living" and "stone" perfectly spaced. He reached into the bottom drawer of the big old wooden desk that served as his projects table as well as for homework, and hauled out a hardly used Uher cassette recorder that somebody had given Tom Benjamin years before. There was a fresh tape already inserted in place, and the power level of the batteries was still sufficiently high.

Jamie pushed the record button and held the mike in front of Teddy. "Testing… Testing… one, two, three, four…" the bear said, making his deep voice sound even more authoritative. "Okay, Jamie, let's play it back." They were both satisfied, so Jamie cleaned the tape. It wouldn't do to have "Okay, Jamie" turn up on it.

"Ready?" Jamie asked.

"Teddy's ready," the bear replied, chuckling at his own joke. Jamie pushed the button again and Teddy cleared his throat. "Good evening, Miss Livingstone," he began. "As you can see from our note, we are very dangerous men…"

When he finished, Jamie fished the cassette out of the recorder and, just to be sure there were no prints, wiped it clean with a spit-moistened Kleenex tissue. He slipped it into the standard sized envelope with the note and sealed the flap. Then he dropped the envelope into a Baggie and twist-tied the top; when that was done, he left the room, carrying the tape recorder in one hand and the *Newsweek* in the other. The recorder went back in his father's desk in the study and the magazine into the garbage, shoved down out of sight along one side of the bag. How terribly easy it had all been, Jamie thought. If the kidnappers on TV were as smart as he and Teddy, they'd never get caught.

And he didn't even mind all that much that he was sexually excited by it all and by the anticipation of what would come of it. Hot images of Miss Livingstone, naked and alone, fearful and helpless, ebbed and flowed before his mind's eye. He was giving the orders, he and Teddy, and she was pleading with them. *Anything, she'd do anything, but please don't hurt the girl...*

"Jamie?" The images evaporated, although the erection remained and his throat felt so thick that he could not even croak a reply.

"Jamie, is that you? I thought you were in bed." Sandy, pulling a robe over her nightie as she came out of the guest room, her room, was cutting off his path as well as his thoughts. "Why, you're still dressed," she said. "Don't you know how late it is?"

"Oh, I was... uh... I was thirsty, so I... uh went down to the kitchen for a glass of milk. I... uh..."

"Well get undressed and get into bed, Jamie. And go to sleep."

He could not tell what it was, but he knew there was something wrong. She seemed angry with him, even more angry than she'd been earlier in the day when she'd caught him watching her sleep. And she seemed, well, scared. *Maybe,* he figured, *she thought I was a burglar or something.*

"And just what were you doing before that, before you went down for milk, if that's what you were doing?" She demanded, the edge still on her voice.

"Nothing. I was..." *Think fast, Jamie.* "I was just drawing pictures. Of the trogs. Wait, I'll show you. He rushed into his room, grabbed a pile of week-old drawing pictures from the top drawer of his desk, and ran back out into the hall before she could follow him in. "See," he said, shoving the pencil sketched into her less-than-willing hands. "This is what they look like. Please like them, Sandy."

She flipped through quickly, without stopping to study

any one page, then handed them back without saying a word. Jamie said, "Well?" with his face, but he didn't get much of an answer, at least not the one he was expecting.

"You draw well, Jamie," she said.

"But what do you think about the trogs, Sandy?"

"I think they look horrible," she said flatly.

He felt tears in his eyes. *What's going on*, he asked himself, *What's the matter, doesn't she like me any more? What did I do to her?*

Sandy saw, and her own expression changed. He could see tears in her eyes now too, but at least there was a smile to go with them. She reached out and touched him lightly on the arm, and he felt good all over—not sexy good, he didn't think, but happy good. Just good.

"I'm sorry, Jamie," she said. "I was thinking about something that was making me really unhappy and I just went and took it out on you. That wasn't fair, and I'm sorry."

Jamie didn't know what to say. A few people had said they were sorry to him before, but it was usually like an "excuse me." They didn't really mean it; they only said it because they were people who said things without thinking about it. But this was the first real apology anybody'd ever made, where he was right and they were wrong and they said so.

"Oh, that's okay, Sandy," he said gallantly, as though he'd spent a lifetime rehearsing for this very moment. "I don't mind, honest. I mean, everybody has their troubles."

"Thank you, Jamie." She put the ends of two fingers to her lips, made a kissing sound, and touched the fingers to his forehead. He felt his face get very red, and he knew that she could see it too, even in the fairly dim light of the hallway. It wasn't that he wanted to lose this moment, but he just didn't know what more he could do with it.

Then the answer came, from somewhere out of the blue, and he broke the spell. "Sandy," he asked urgently, "my friends, the trogs, what do you think they eat?"

"Oh, Christ, Jamie, I..." Then, instantly, her eyes softened, and she looked down into his face for a few seconds before she replied, her tone more subdued. "I really can't answer that, Jamie. Have you... uh... offered them any kinds of food?"

He shook his head. "I never thought of it until now. Isn't that weird, Sandy? We've been friends for nearly three months now, and I never brought them food. Do you know what trogs eat?"

"Well," she said, sounding like she really wanted to help, "what do you like to eat best, I mean, for a treat?"

"Chocolate bars," he replied, very excited at the possibility of a solution to his new problem. "*Three Musketeers*, especially. That's what I'll do. Tomorrow. I'll see if they like chocolate bars. Oh, thank you, Sandy!"

He hugged her, quickly and clumsily, and ran off to his room. She stood there for a little while, and the worry returned to her face.

"Constable," Margaret Livingstone said with enough edge on her voice to establish that she was at least half-serious, "if you don't hurry up and get your butt out of here, I'm calling the police."

"Please, Margaret, just a few more minutes."

"David, it's one thirty in the morning!"

"I'm almost done," he mumbled, putting the fifth-last photostat face down on a stack of paper that had grown to a thickness of about an inch-and-a-half. He read quickly down the page in front of him, stopping every few moments to make tiny scrawls in his official police notebook. "Police business," he repeated for perhaps the sixth or seventh time that night and the fourth time in the past hour.

"Oh sure! And tell me, Inspector Dupin, whom do you

really suspect in the murders of the Rue Morgue? My money's on the trained ape."

Other than something muffled and unintelligible, no response. *Oh well*, she sighed, and made herself another drink. This time, she didn't even bother to ask if he wanted one and just automatically filled his coffee cup instead. He was having one of his self-denial days, working like hell to do penance for his sins of the night before.

It's amazing, she thought, *how even the most staunch of ex-Catholics are never really free of that need.*

She left him alone with his stats and his notes and tiptoed down the hall to stand outside Abergail's room, listening to the breathing patterns through the door and assuring herself that her niece was still asleep. Abergail had been very upset earlier, when she'd returned home from her modern dance class and found this *man*—David had changed into faded jeans and an old University of Wisconsin T-shirt before arriving in the living room. She hadn't said anything, but Margaret had seen it in her eyes. And it had made her feel guilty. (*See, Margaret, you don't have to be Catholic!*)

At first she'd thought Abergail's distress had been due to the fact that she'd allowed David to come over, instead of sticking to her guns and delivering the material to his place. Abergail, for her part, had been polite, but cold and formal, and had made excuses to go to bed long before her usual time.

With Abergail's chill fresh in her mind, and with David incommunicado for all intents and purposes anyway, Margaret began to think about the life she'd created for herself and her niece. It was not the first time she'd brought her isolation from men into serious doubt, but she was beginning to feel a certain amount of urgency about her future now, more so than before. Being with David again, last night and again tonight, had set her off; but it wasn't just that. In two weeks, Abergail would be thirteen years old, and she had been menstruating for three months, but her interest in boys remained absolutely zero. In fact, it was worse than just simple lack of interest: there was hostility there, both spoken and unspoken.

Margaret could understand her niece's hatred of kids like Freddy Hoekstra, who was a bully and a showoff, and of that disgusting Benjamin child.

Or, Margaret stopped and asked herself, *do I just understand why she hates Jamie because I hate him so much? And, for that matter, why do I hate him? Because of the picture? Well, that's part of it, but the truth is, he gives me the creeps. The way he looks at me like... like... a dirty old man. He makes me want to get into a boiling hot bath and scrub myself with a brush. One thing I know for sure and that is that I wouldn't want to be anywhere around him when he grows up.*

But no, Agergail's attitude to all boys and, for that matter, to all men, seemed to her to be pretty unhealthy.

What if she ends up a lesbian, Margaret asked herself, *will it be my fault? her? Was my so-called "sacrifice" really for her good or was it just some kind of irrational reaction to my sister's death, an ill-conceived decision I was too stubborn to change? David's sitting in there, and he looks so very beautiful to me and God help me there's nothing I want more than to go in and take him by the hand and lead him to my bedroom.*

Then why don't you?

Abergail. I'm worried about Abergail. What if she woke up, what if she heard?

Then go back to his place with him.

I can't. I can't leave her alone.

Are you sure it's for Abergail's sake?

No, I'm not. But I can't do anything right away. I have to talk to her about it. We have to talk it over. I have to undo what I've done, what I might have done, more slowly. Tomorrow. No, she's going out tomorrow night. Maybe on the weekend.

When she returned to the living room, David was

carrying around the last of his coffee in his left hand and stuffing his notebook into the rear pocket of his jeans with his right. He was bleary-eyed, but his smile was just glorious. Her belly went *pang*.

"So," she said, gathering up the dirty dishes and the ashtrays, "are the forces of law and order any closer to their inevitable triumph?"

He laughed. "Let's just say that my suspicions remain unconfirmed." Then, more seriously, "Margaret, I know that you think I'm letting my imagination run away with me, and that a cop, of all people, should not allow that to happen. But..." He reached for her cigarettes, but she brushed his hand away, took two from the pack, lit them and passed one over to him. "Love your lipstick," he said, and then began coughing as a little of the smoke accidentally found its way into his windpipe. When he finished choking, he picked up again on his original thought. "But, Margaret, there have been some very strange things happening on that Whately place, as I told you. And tonight I found at least one more."

She glanced down at her watch.

"Just a few more minutes, Margaret," he apologized.

"Oh, go ahead," she said. "My evening's all shot to hell anyway."

"Anyway," he said, looking at his own watch and making a surprised face, "did you know that during the mid-Thirties, when they were quarrying that red granite deposit out there near the Whately place, there was an outbreak of dead livestock in these parts?"

"No, of course I didn't know that. And, David, your roots are showing."

"What?" he said, uncomprehending.

"You said, 'these parts,' David. When are you going to start spitting tobacco and predicting changes in the weather?"

But he was just too wound up to be either embarrassed or

sidetracked. "It happened in the late fall. Mostly dairy cattle, but there were a few sheep and horses too. They found about fifteen carcasses in all, with their throats slashed and most of the meat eaten off them. It was cold, so they were in pretty good shape for carcasses—but because the ground was frozen, there were no footprints around them. And do you know what else? The three farmers who lost the livestock told the police—my father was a young cop then, and his name is mentioned in the story—that they'd lost more than just fifteen cows. There were twenty-five head of cattle, two horses, and six or seven sheep not accounted for. That means more than half of that livestock just disappeared. Oh, and another thing: there were deer in the woods then, whitetails, and four or five of them, including this huge buck, were killed and eaten in the same way as the cattle and sheep." He stopped to let his discovery sink in.

"Wolves," she said. "Or wild dogs. David, just what the hell are you trying to get at, what are you trying to tell me? That there are monsters in the woods? Sasquatches? Well, where the hell have they been for the last forty-five years, why hasn't anybody ever seen them? Come on, David, this Whately's Copse or whatever it's called is on the edge of a good-sized town that's been here for a hundred years: it's not some rain forest in the African interior. Are you, David Bentley, a fairly intelligent man and a policeman, going to lay some silly superstition on me? If you are, stop right now, because I don't want to hear it. And, what's more…"

Abergail was standing in the doorway from the hall, rubbing at her eyes, her red hair sticking up all over the place. "Aunt Margaret," she said, taking a step backward out of the light, "I heard shouting. I thought something bad was happening."

Awake now, she turned toward David and glared.

Oh Christ. "No, it's okay, honey, it was all my fault. I just got too worked up about something Constable Bentley was saying. You go back to bed and I'll be in in a few minutes." Abergail shot David a look that was so full of hate and anger that he had to turn away from it. Then she disappeared down the dark hall and they could hear a door slam.

"David, you'd better go."

"Okay, but first, let me defend myself. I'll be quick"

No, she thought. "Yes," she said, "but do hurry.

"Right. Okay, there were no wolves spotted that fall, and besides, wolves only come near civilized areas when they're starving, which means late winter, usually. There were no wild dogs, and no cougars either: no cougar could do all that killing, and no cougar would take one busk deer if he didn't have to. Also, the killing of the livestock apparently ended with the first snowfall, which was about the same time as the water in the quarry froze over. And, for your information, Whately's Copse might as well be in the middle of Africa, because nobody goes there and nobody has for a hundred years—except the very brave or the very foolish." He realized that his voice was rising, and that Margaret was looking from him to her watch to the darkened hallway, so he whispered the rest. "Margaret, I'm not suggesting that anything supernatural went on out there, or is going on out there, and I'm certainly not suggesting that good old Reverend Morley and all the other folks who've disappeared were eaten by demons. But… but I'm telling you this—and I beg you never to mention it to a living soul—when I was down in that hole, Margaret, I could feel eyes on me. I didn't see anything, I didn't smell anything, and I didn't hear anything. But I felt them. I felt I had to get out of there, or I was going to die."

She couldn't help herself; she reached over and took his hand, which was cold to the touch and trembling. "David," she said, ever-so-softly, "I think you need that drink now. I'll just see to Abergail, and I'll be right back."

She wondered, as she left him slumped there in the chair,

what he was really going through, to make him so suddenly obsessed with this ridiculous notion.

When she returned, he was asleep. And while she didn't want to wake him, she did and sent him on his way.

On the weekend, she reaffirmed to herself, *I will definitely have that talk with Abergail.*

CHAPTER FOURTEEN

SANDY HAD WAKENED with a vicious headache and even now, at twelve forty-five in the afternoon, after four aspirins and an ice bag, it wasn't a damn bit better, if anything it was worse. She wondered how genuine migraine sufferers kept from killing themselves. Breakfast with Jamie—bacon and eggs far inferior to his batch of the previous day —had seemed like it would never end. Jamie, oblivious to her expression and mood, had babbled on happily about the trogs and what a great idea she'd had about feeding them chocolate bars and, yes that's just what he'd do on his way home from school, and...

Oh yes, she suddenly realized, that's where he was: feeding chocolate bars to troglodytes. She was as embarrassed as she could feel under the circumstances that she was just noticing his absence half an hour after he was imposed to be home for lunch. Yeah, he's out feeding his monsters. She wished Allan would come, and she wished that Barbara and Tom Benjamin would hurry up and find back home, and she wished most of all at that very moment that her head would stop hurting. She had even tried talking to herself about this whole mess, this whole insane deteriorating mess, but she was just feeling too mean to listen. Shit and double shit!

"Hiya, Sandy!" The happy little shout was immediately followed by the cannon-crack of the screen door slamming.

"Goddamnit, Jamie!"

Instantly she was ashamed of herself, and as she watched the bright smile dissolve into trembling lips and little confused tears, she began to crumble. Somehow, as everything began to grow gray and hazy before her eyes, she managed to sit down on a kitchen chair. And then, face buried in her hands, she wept. "Oh Jamie, Jamie!" she sobbed, "I'm so sorry, I'm so terribly sorry!"

Blindly she reached out for his hand, but it was Jamie who reacted first. He was standing beside her, one arm over her shoulders, squeezing too tightly but the only way he knew how. He stroked her arm with his other hand, and through his own pain and bewilderment, he tried to comfort her with soothing words that she only half-heard.

Finally she could feel the spell ending, and slowly she lifted her head and turned to look into Jamie's still-frightened eyes. What she saw only served to make her hate herself even more, and if she had been able to do so, she probably would have begun crying again; but she had nothing left, nothing except the still-excruciating throb in her head and a terrible sense of helplessness. She had begun to realize—*when? last night? a few days ago? this morning?*—that for the first time in her young life, she was losing control of her own situation, and she feared as well, thanks to four years of psychology, that she was close to, if not in fact caught up in, the early stages of an emotional breakdown.

But why? What had happened to make her feel this way? Jamie? *Come on, Sandy, what the hell has he done, anyway? Looked at you funny? Well isn't that too goddamned bad! So he has imaginary friends—okay, imaginary monsters—that he talks to in the woods. What has that got to do with you? Admit it, Sandy, you just don't like him. Even though his mother warned you, you wouldn't believe her. She said that nobody liked Jamie, and you figured she was just making excuses for herself, didn't you? You figured you were so goddamned smart and so goddamned under- standing and all, that you could be this boy's friend. Do you know what your problem is, Sandy? You're arrogant. You think you can make everything you touch work, and that you can change people into what you think they should be, just because you're you. What the hell did you expect from this boy, anyhow? That he'd just suddenly become normal, become a model child just through sheer exposure to your presence?*

"Jamie," she said, unwilling to look him in the face again, at least for a little while longer, "I'm just having a hard time I can't explain and I'm putting it all on you. I'm sorry and I'll try to stop. I know I keep saying the same thing to you, over and over, that I always seem to be apologizing, but I promise this will be it."

"Don't worry about it," said that unsettling deep voice that she'd heard once before. She shifted backward involun- tarily at the sound of it, and when she turned her head toward the boy, she was deeply afraid of what she might see. But it was just Jamie, still looking confused and concerned. For a long moment their eyes locked, and then they each managed a little smile, mutually acknowledging that this crisis, at least, was over.

"Look what I brought you," Jamie said. In his hand was a crumpled *Three Musketeers* bar, still in its wrapper. "They didn't like the chocolate bars, Sandy. One of them tried to eat one and he spit it out, and then they all got grunting at one another, and they went away where I couldn't see them."

"Oh?" she said. *No matter what happens from here on in, you are going to go along with it, and that's that. Unless he tries to take you there. You cannot go there.*

"But don't worry, Sandy. We'll figure something out."

"Yeah, sure, Jamie."

"Maybe Teddy'll know. I'll..." His hand went to his mouth suddenly, as if to stuff the words back in. Before she could read the new expression on his face, he turned his back to her and walked toward the sink, where he poured himself a glass of water. *Who's Teddy? He's never mentioned a Teddy before? Is it the bear, that stuffed bear? Does he talk to that, too? Oh, my God!*

"Teddy's a kid at school," he said quickly, his back still to her. "He's only in the sixth grade, but he's kind of my friend."

"I thought... I thought..." Her mouth was so dry she could only croak ineffectually. "I was the only one who knew about the... uh... troglodytes?"

"Oh," Jamie said, facing her now and very composed, "you are. But I might tell him, if that's okay with you, Sandy. I mean, it is *our* secret."

She was sure he was lying, but she just didn't care. "Go ahead," she said. Then she rose slowly and dragged herself to the refrigerator. She took out two Saran-covered bowls and carried them to the table. "Now we'd better eat lunch, don't you think? You're due back at school in half an hour."

He devoured his tuna fish salad greedily. When he left, closing the screen door carefully behind him and glancing back to ensure that his consideration had not gone unnoticed, Sandy spooned the rest of her lunch into the garbage can and stuffed their bowls and milk glasses into the dishwasher.

Then, for no reason she could be sure of, other than the fact that Jamie's bed needed making, she went up to his room. The bear was propped up against the headboard, its button-eyes staring at her as she came through the door. *Sandy, don't be stupid!* She lifted the bear off the bed and sat him on the desk while she stripped away the sheets and pillow cases and made a bundle for the washing machine. She could still feel the eyes on her, but she was damned if she was going to show it. This *was* Teddy, she was sure of it. But he was only a stuffed toy, a pajama bag, and if…

Her hand touched something slick and cold as she straightened the mattress. She pulled out in old, tattered copy of *Playboy*. In spite of herself, she smiled, A hidden-away copy of *Playboy* was such a terribly normal thing; it was almost reassuring.

She flipped through it absently, then carefully returned it to its rightful place between the mattress and the box spring. Then she picked up the bundle of linen and started for the door. Inexplicably she turned and considered the staring bear. "You," she murmured, "and that magazine. It just doesn't make any sense."

JAMIE HAD NEVER BEEN able to fully come to terms with the fact that the butcher shop was called "Fruitman's Fine Meats". A man named Fruitman, he'd reasoned the first day he'd ever been in the place with Barbara, should be selling, well, fruit. Barbara had explained that many names—Benjamin not among them, that she knew of—originated with what people did, and that probably one of Mr. Fruitman's ancestors had in fact sold fruit. Jamie understood, but he still found it very, curious.

"So, my young Mr. Benjamin," Sol Fruitman said, wiping his hands on his bloodied apron, "what can I do for you today? The chops are on special, and I'll tell you, they look so good, I could almost eat them myself."

Jamie didn't get it and his face showed it.

"I am a Jew, Mr. Benjamin, not a very good Jew but a Jew nonetheless. I sell pork, I sell bacon, I sell ham and I sell chops, but I do not eat them. It goes with being a Jew… you don't understand, do you?"

Jamie shook his head.

"No," the butcher said, "why should you? Even I don't, sometimes, so why should you, my handsome little goy? But tell me, what can I do for you?"

Jamie read the red and white plastic price tags in the refrigerated glass case, and he thought about the $5.48 he had in his pocket. There certainly wasn't much he could buy for that. Some of the stuff cost more than that for a pound. But he didn't want to take too long; he didn't want to make Mr. Fruitman mad at him because, well, Mr. Fruitman always treated him nice and never yelled at him and never told him to get out of the store. The hamburger was selling for $1.59 a pound, and Jamie quickly calculated mentally that he could get about three and-a-half pounds for the money he had, and that seemed like a lot.

"I'll take the hamburger," he said, pointing through the glass.

"A pound?" Mr. Fruitman smiled.

"No… uh… can you give me… uh… about five dollars and forty-eight cents worth, please?

"No sooner said than done, Mt. Benjamin." Fruitman began scooping the ground meat onto a piece of brown wrapping paper. "Your parents are planning a barbecue?" he asked as he dropped the purchase on the scale.

Jamie saw that the needle was just touching the four-pound mark, but instead of shoveling some of the meat back into the tray in the showcase, Mr. Fruitman wrapped it quickly, tied it with string, wrote $5.48 on the package, and handed it to the boy.

Jamie started to protest, but Mr. Fruitman put a finger to his lips. "Our little secret," he said. "Enjoy it in good health."

"Thank you." Jamie said, handing over his handful of change and crumpled dollar bills. "Cross my heart and hope to die." Happily, with a wave, he rushed out of the store.

Because he was moving too fast, by the time he saw the wheelchair, it was too late. His foot caught in the right wheel and he went sprawling along the sidewalk, ripping skin off his elbows, and banging his left knee painfully. The package flew out of his hands, struck mushily against a parked car, and dropped into the gutter.

"My God, what was that?" he heard a familiar and hateful voice say behind him. Miss Oliphant, that frigging Miss Oliphant! Shakily he dragged himself to his feet, tested the knee to discover that it would still hold him, and turned to face what he knew was coming.

"It's that terrible Benjamin boy again, Emma," the other woman said. The other woman was named Louise, and according to Barbara, Louise was Miss Oliphant's paid companion. That had made sense to Jamie, because he was sure that nobody as rotten as Miss Oliphant could get a companion for free.

She was blind and she was crippled, and he knew that he was supposed to feel sorry for her, but he didn't. She was like the wicked witch in *The Wizard Of Oz*, and Jamie wanted to believe that some day she'd suffer the same awful fate. It was Miss Oliphant who had gotten his bike taken away, just because there had been a little accident. He hadn't meant run into her, but Tom and Barbara hadn't believed him. Besides, Barbara had said it wasn't because of the accident, it was because of all those terrible names Jamie had called Miss Oliphant and Louise. Jamie could not remember doing that, but Barbara had said—as she did so often—that he has a "convenient" memory.

Still, if he had said anything, it was only after Miss Oliphant had slapped his face, he was sure of that. He'd been trying to say he was sorry, and then Louise was shouting at him, and so was Miss Oliphant, and he'd started talking louder and she'd hit him. She couldn't have seen him, he knew, because she was blind, but she reached out and hit him hard anyway.

Not again! He turned and limped to the package in the

gutter and, without even inspecting it for rips and tears, gathered it up and started away.

"Come back here young man! Come back here this very instant!" That was Louise's voice. He pretended not to hear and continued to limp away. Blood was dribbling from his left elbow, and it was pounding in his temples. His ears burned, and he could feel rage beginning to bubble up from somewhere deep in his chest. *Don't stop, Jamie, whatever you do! Don't stop, don't say anything, don't listen!*

But he couldn't help hearing: "Well, it seems that I'll have to have another talk with those parents of his. And if that doesn't do any good, then by God, I'll call the police. He should be put away, that boy!'

Some day, Miss Oliphant, *I'll put you away.*

CHAPTER FIFTEEN

JAMIE CALLED OUT TWICE, identifying himself, and waited. In a few minutes he could hear the pig-grunting sounds—before the scratching, this time coming from way off somewhere under the earth and growing progressively louder. Then he saw the yellow eyes, looking up at him, and there was a perceptible change in the nature of the grunts. They sounded almost friendly now, and that pleased Jamie a lot. He'd had a puppy once, but it hadn't been a very happy puppy except with him; after a few weeks, Tom had taken it away, telling Jamie that the dog was sick, but Jamie knew Tom had wanted it out of there just because it kept peeing and pooping on the floor. It had been the only pet Jamie had ever been allowed—the toads and the snakes weren't really pets, although he didn't know just what they actually were. He had never forgotten the happy loving sounds that animals could make.

The trogs, his friends, were glad to see him.

He started to unwrap the hamburger, then changed his mind. It would get all dirty down there. So he retied the filing and dropped the whole package. The shadowy figures melted away from it at first, and Jamie sensed their suspicion.

"No," he said softly, "don't be afraid. It's food. To eat. I know you didn't like the chocolate bars, but this is different."

They understood! He felt triumphant, as one, then another of the troglodytes approached the package, sniffing at it, touching it with those talon-like fingers. Then one of them—the leader, Jamie decided—lifted it up and held it. He looked up at Jamie and growled something that Jamie took to mean either "What is it?' or "Thank you." He tore away the paper and string and took a handful of the soft, reddish meat and held it to his nose. Then, to Jamie's astonishment and pleasure, he shoved the whole handful into his mouth.

Jamie did not know what he expected to happen next, but it was certainly not what *did* happen. After the leader had noisily chewed and swallowed the meat, he did not grab another handful. Instead, he *offered it around*. No, there was no mistake. The leader was slowly turning in a circle, and the others were taking portions and stuffing them into their mouths. When the other four had taken their share—and that's what it had seemed like to Jamie, that they had taken almost equal shares—the leader looked up at Jamie and grunted something that Jamie took to be either another "Thank you," or an "Is there any more?"

"Oh, don't worry," Jamie replied. "Now that I know you like meat, I'll bring you lots of food."

"Yes, Miss Oliphant, I'll be sure to tell them. No, Miss Oliphant, I won't forget. Fine. Thank you for calling. 'Bye now." Sandy replaced the receiver and added, for her own ears only, "Fuck you, Miss Oliphant." If this was the kind of shit Jamie had to put up with all the time, it was no wonder he was half-nuts, it was no wonder that he talked to teddy bears and imaginary creatures in the forest. For the moment, at least, she was back on Jamie's side and feeling guilty that she'd ever left it.

She mixed up a pitcher of her famous limeade and put it in the refrigerator. She knew that would please him. Then she went out on the back porch and felt the sheets and towels on the line and, satisfied, she began to reel them in.

"Hi," Jamie said, coming around the corner of the house.

"Hi yourself," she said back, matching his happy tone. Then, "Jamie, you're bleeding! Look at your elbow!"

He studied one elbow, then the other, as if trying to figure out just where and how he'd gotten hurt. "Oh yeah," he said, "I was running and I fell."

"Was that before or after you ran into the woman in the wheelchair?" It wasn't an accusation, although she knew it might have come out sounding that way. But no, she didn't want to catch him out in a lie, to embarrass him, so she continued rapidly, "I had a call from a Miss Oliphant a little while ago…"

"Oh?" he said, hanging his head. "I guess you'll have to tell Tom and Barbara when they get back?'

"No, Jamie. No, I won't. They may find out about it—I'm sure that old woman will see to that—but I'm not going to say a thing. You can count on it."

"Oh, Sandy!" he said, the tears of happiness welling in his eyes. "Oh, Sandy, thank you so much! Nobody's ever believed me before, that it wasn't my fault. I love you, Sandy!"

He came close and hugged her, and she tried to hug him back, but her body was tense and unwilling. Still, she managed to put her arms around his shoulders and to ease herself away without really telegraphing her reluctance. "I… uh… I think you're pretty special too, Jamie," she said, honestly. "Now let me have a look at those scrapes. We'd better get them cleaned up before they get infected. Why don't you go up and hop in the bathtub and soak them for a while? That'll get rid of the soreness, too, probably."

He looked her right in the eyes, and she could read absolutely nothing into his faint little smile. "Will you come up later and wash my back?" he asked shyly.

Something told her no, but she was not disposed to listen. Sure, why not? She'd bathed kids before, and even though Jamie was older than any of the others, he was still a kid. But she had to set a few rules. "Aren't you a little old for that?" she asked, giving him the chance to either back out or suggest a compromise. He chose the latter.

"I'll put some of Barbara's bubble bath in. You won't see anything. Will you wash my back, Sandy, *will you?*"

"Sure, Jamie, I'll be up in a few minutes. I'll even bring you a surprise."

"Great," he said, bounding past her; then he stopped and caught the screen door before it slammed.

SHE WAITED outside the closed bathroom door until the water stopped running, and his little groan informed her that he was safely in the tub. Even then she moved cautiously. But his disarming smile and the double handful of suds he held up were sufficient proof that the offending parts of his body were indeed safely obscured from her sight.

As he sipped the limeade she'd brought him—the surprise—she sat on the closed toilet lid trying to figure out just how she fit in with Jamie's immediate plans. She was certain that he was sexually attracted to her, and she knew that in his own way he was in love with her. No, it couldn't be any more than a little boy's love, but to him it was real and important. And no, she reviewed her words and actions of the previous few days, *I haven't done anything to encourage him.* Which made her feel only slightly less uncomfortable. In the beginning her instincts and her reasoning had been pretty much in agreement so far as Jamie was concerned. Now they were not, and she did not know which to trust. She still could not shake the vague, growing feeling that there was something menacing about Jamie.

He held up the soapy washcloth to her, and she had to make a decision. She saw that he recognized her hesitation, and she instantly felt caught out. Without a word she took the cloth from him and began to move it carefully over the soft, unpimpled skin of his back.

"Oh, Sandy, " he said, closing his eyes, "that feels great!"

CHIEF BECKER TORREY had listened patiently and attentively for more than an hour while David told and retold all he had learned about the Whately family and Whately's Copse, but now the Chief was starting to sneak glances at his watch. While police work never stops, policemen, even chiefs, *do* get the urge to stop now and then, especially late on Friday afternoons when the work seems to be pretty well in hand. Torrey wished he had never told David about his great grandmother or his open-mindedness toward things not readily explicable. If he hadn't said all that, it would have been easy to cut off David in mid-flight and tell him to keep his investigation a little more conventional. However...

"Well, David," he sighed, "that's all very interesting, but what does it take us to? Unless I've misunderstood you, you're at a dead end. And unless you've got something more solid, I don't have much choice other than to tell you to put the Morley case on the back burner and get onto something else. McLachlan's got that string of break-ins, and Cogan needs some door-to-door help on that indecent assault over on Fourth Street, just for starters."

"But, Beck," David protested, "there's something going on out there in that clearing in the Copse. I'm sure of it."

"That's what you've been saying for an hour, David, but you haven't told me what. Now let's just get off the subject, okay? If anything substantial turns up, you go back on the case, otherwise, it's finished. Now, let's get over to the club, while we still have a chance at a court."

JAMIE AND TEDDY watched from the window, secretly, as Sandy and her "friend," Allan, embraced on the front walk. She had asked Jamie, while she bandaged his elbow, if he minded if this Allan came over. But she had made it sound as if Allan was coming, whether Jamie liked it or not. He had minded, but had nodded anyway.

"Looks like more than a friend to me, Jamie," Teddy said, a nasty little nudge in his voice.

"She said she didn't love him," Jamie replied, not so convinced now, but trying not to show it.

"She's kissing him on the lips. And look, he's touching her on the ass!"

"Yeah, but you look. She's moving his hand away."

"Jamie, forget it. To her you're just a little kid. She doesn't love you. I bet she doesn't even—"

Jamie swung blindly, knocking Teddy off the dresser and across the room. The bear landed face-down on the floor by the closet door and then, suddenly, Jamie had him by the neck, pushing him up against the wall.

"Fuck you, Teddy, fuck you, you rotten cunt-prick bear!" The tears were streaming down his face, but his mouth was a bared-tooth snarl. "She loves me, I told you, you fuckface shit! She does love me and when I get older I'm going to marry her and you can go to hell!"

Then a very strange thing happened. Instead of fighting

back, Teddy just looked back at Jamie with soft, understanding eyes and said, "Okay, Jamie, maybe you're right. Maybe she does love you. And you know what? I bet she was just kissing that guy to make you jealous. Sure, that's what it was. She figured you'd be watching and she did it to make you jealous."

"Are you sure, Teddy? Do you really think that?"

"Sure, Jamie. What else could it be?"

Jamie hugged the bear and then sat him gently on the bed. "I have to go and meet Allan," he said. "I promised I would. I'll be right back. And Teddy?"

"Yes, Jamie?"

"Thank you for understanding, thanks for seeing it my way… And I'm really sorry I hit you like that."

"No problem. But hurry back. Remember, this is the night we pay Miss Livingstone a visit." The unhealthy gleam returned to his eyes, and Jamie laughed.

"Well," Allan said, removing his sunglasses and hanging them over the rearview mirror, "you know the literature about as well as I do. So you know that it isn't uncommon for children to have surprisingly extensive fantasy lives. And for boys especially, holes are common elements of those fantasies, holes with witches and trolls and monsters in them. And you don't have to have read much Freud to interpret what that means, do you? I mean, I have a certain fantasy about such things myself…"

"Allan, for Christ's sake, don't make jokes. Not now. I'm too upset." She had listened to herself recount the previous *few* days' events with a sinking heart. It had sounded even dumber when spoken aloud to another person; and Allan had given her no sympathy whatsoever. From the time they'd left the house, with Jamie's strangely-enthusiastic blessing, he'd done little more than make her feel what she'd been feeling for days, only more so. "You're turning that kid into an obsession," he'd said.

"I am not," she'd replied.

"Then forgot about him," he'd said.

"I... I can't," she'd admitted.

They were parked by the river, well upstream from the paper mill, where the water still ran relatively unpolluted. The sun was behind the tall pines on the opposite bank now, and the light was dying. The warm hum of the day had ended, and the night sounds of frogs and crickets had not yet begun, so around them there was silence. She broke it. "Allan?"

"Shh," he whispered. He put his hand out to her, and she took it, draping it over her shoulder as she slid across the seat and buried her face in his chest. She cried softly, and he stroked her hair until she was finished. "Allan," she said finally, "what's the matter with me?"

"I can't answer that, Sandy," he said, turning her face to his and studying it carefully. "Probably nothing terminal, though. You found yourself involved with this kid, probably because he seemed to be a loser. I won't say that's been a pattern with you, sweetheart, but what you have to accept in yourself is that you're vulnerable to that kind of thing. Ask yourself why you got into psych in the first place, why you want to do clinical work." He paused for à moment, ran his tongue over his mustache and then completed his thought. "What you really have to ask yourself—and right now seems as good a time as any—is whether or not you can handle the work emotionally. Maybe this experience with Jamie is a good thing, in a way. Maybe it's showing you that your strength is not in dealing directly with people. You've got yourself too involved, and while that may be very admirable under some circumstances, I'm convinced that no clinical psychologist can survive that way."

She started to answer, but he cut her off. "Don't. Just think about it for a while. I may be dead wrong, but you asked me so I told you. Arguing won't help."

"But Allan," she protested weakly, "the boy…"

"He'll make it or he won't. A week from today he'll just be a fresh memory to you, and a month from today he'll seem a long, long way off. As he will be."

Her face was still demanding an answer, and he knew it.

"Okay," he said, turning the ignition key and reaching down for the shift lever, "I'll tell you what I'll do. Tomorrow, if he wants, I'll spend some time with him. I'll see if I think your assessment is correct, and if I agree, then I'll come back next week and talk to the parents with you. Is that a deal?'

"Dr. Dressen, I think you're terrific!"

"Don't call me doctor, it's bad luck. And stop doing *that*, for Christ's sake, you're making me crazy!" She laughed happily and did as she was told. After a while.

CHAPTER SIXTEEN

IF MARGARET LIVINGSTONE had not been the disciplined woman that she was and prided herself to be, the choice between the bathtub and the black Danskin exercise suit hanging on the hook beside it would have been easy. Only a few hours sleep the night before, thanks to David Bentley, followed by a particularly long day in the library, disposed her much more toward a good soak and a good sleep than a sweaty half-hour of ballet exercises. What's more, Abergail was still out at the school dance, which meant that nobody would ever know if she skipped her workout just this once.

Margaret examined her naked body in the full-length bathroom mirror. Everything was fine until she got to her thighs. She pinched at them and made a face. Then, with a sign, she reached for the Danskin and pulled it on. Back in her bedroom she switched on the lights, shoved a London Symphony 8-track of *Swan Lake* into the stereo, and flicked on the power. She took a deep, professional breath and went up on point. Then another breath, as she lifted her right leg straight up and out, describing a perfect arc with the downward-turned toes. She brought it slowly back, maintaining near-flawless balance.

"Oh, shit," she muttered. Who the hell was ringing her doorbell at ten thirty at night? Abergail? No, she knew the door was left open for her. David? If it was, she'd kill him. Margaret grabbed a white terry cloth robe from a hook in the bathroom and had almost struggled into it by the time she reached the front door. With all of the impatience she felt, she flung the door open and came face to face with nobody. What the hell was this? Did some stupid kid think it was Halloween? Then she saw at her feet the envelope with her name so neatly pasted on it, and she thought: *Jamie Benjamin! If this is another of his sickie games, by God, it'll be his last!*

She lifted the envelope tentatively. It held something heavier than a note, she realized, heavier than another of the brat's filthy disgusting pictures. She returned to the bedroom and held it up to the bright light.

There was a cassette tape inside, along with a note. Her first impulse was to call David, but she stifled it. The cutout, pasted-down "miss living stone" on the envelope pricked her curiosity as much as it disturbed her.

Hands trembling, she cut away one end of the envelope neatly with her manicure scissors and let the contents slide onto the bed. She picked up the note first and read it.

"Oh my God! Oh no, oh no, not Abergail! Oh my God, no!" She began to shiver violently, and red mist swirled before her eyes; she couldn't breathe; something bitter and cold was trying to force itself up into her throat; she felt herself slipping away, and she grabbed for the dresser and held on.

Outside in the protective darkness of the night and the thick hedge, two pairs of eyes, one icy blue and the other black, glowed with excitement. "This is going to be even better than we thought," blue eyes whispered. "Hmmm" black eyes replied.

Meanwhile Margaret had recovered herself enough to pick up the tape from the bed, she took it to her desk, dropped it into her Sony, and pushed the start butted Then, with a look of pure hatred on her face, she walked to the picture window, as the note had commanded and stood there, hands on hips. Whoever was out there would not see her cry and cringe and beg for mercy. If they had Abergail—and she was no longer certain they did, although she couldn't take that chance—she would do anything they asked. But not until they asked it. She would not give them that pleasure.

Suddenly, after what seemed a long, long time, she heard the voice, and despite her resolve, her body jerked and her eyes widened and the trembling began again. *"Good evening, Miss Livingstone, as you can see from our note, we are very desperate men..."*

Oh my God! She had hardly heard the words. It was the voice, a terrible deep voice, a voice that could only belong to someone unspeakably evil. Somewhere in her horrified, confused, and disbelieving mind, she apologized to Jamie Benjamin. This was not the voice of a boy, any boy, this was the voice of a madman!

"...and we are holding your niece, Abergail Buhl, in a nice, clean, safe place. We have not harmed one hair of her head, Miss Livingstone. At least, not yet. But we have another place for her, Miss Livingstone, and that one is not so nice and safe and clean. Oh, the rats like it, but then, it's their home. Are you paying attention, Miss Livingstone?"

"Yes," she said, unaware that she was talking to a tape recorder, unaware of everything except the unutterable evil of the voice and the almost unbearable terror that was coursing through her.

"Fine, Miss Livingstone, as long as you know. Now listen carefully and do as we ask, and your niece will be released immediately. Nod if you understand. And remember, we are watching."

She did as she was told. She was beginning to feel a limpness now, a sensation of no longer being there, of not being anywhere. The room, the window, the backyard, and whoever was out there all began to fade away. Margaret felt a strange, not unpleasant warmth, first in her feet and toes, and then her arms and legs, and finally the rest of her. The voice on the tape was the only reality, and even it seemed far away, like an echo of itself.

"Take off your clothes; Miss Livingstone. Now!"

She slid the straps of the Danskin over her shoulders and extracted her arms. Then without ceremony, she just pulled the suit down and stepped out of it. She was only vaguely concerned that she was standing naked in a window for the pleasure of some people out there in the darkness, some people who had… uh… oh, yes, they had Abergail.

"Now, Miss Livingstone, we want you to grab your tits and squeeze them. You have such lovely tits, Miss Livingstone. Much nicer than Abergail's."

Wherever she'd been, suddenly she was back. "I'll kill you, you fucking bastard!" she shrieked into the darkness. "So help me God, if you've harmed her, if you've even looked at her, I'll find you and I'll kill you myself! Ill.

"Aunt Margaret! What are you doing?"

Abergail?

"Aunt Margaret?"

She turned slowly, not even thinking about covering herself, not able to feel shame or anger or any other emotion other than sweet, so very sweet, relief. "You're all right?' she asked in a broken whisper. "You weren't harmed?"

The girl just shook her head, and that, plus the look of disbelief on her face, answered all of Margaret's immediate questions. Satisfied, with a little smile on her face, she crumpled to the floor.

❦

Slipping through the familiar backyards of his neighborhood with Teddy riding happily in the linen laundry bag, Jamie returned home from his adventure full of triumph. The juices of impending manhood pulsed through his body, thrilled his brain, and engorged his penis. Though it was impossible to run, or even walk quickly, that was a small price to pay.

Sandy still wasn't home. He sensed her absence as he stood in the shadows of the elms across the street, assuring himself that there were no cars, no strollers, no neighbors sitting out on their lawns or porches, nobody to take note of his sudden and suspicious appearance. Satisfied, he crossed to the safety of his own house and let himself in the back door. While he stood there in the darkness and confirmed that he and Teddy were alone in the house, he became increasingly aware of his own heavy, unnatural breathing, and the growing, not-unpleasant pain in his groin. With unneeded silence, he crept up the stairs to his room and closed the door. Then he opened the linen bag and brought out Teddy, holding him at arm's length for a few moments of shared, unspoken happiness before sitting him down gently on the bed.

"We did it, Teddy. We did it!" he said, his voice a raspy whisper. "Did you see her face? And the way she played with her tits? It was really great, wasn't it, Teddy? Just like we planned, just like we figured."

The bear's eyes seemed to smile dreamily. "Yes, Jamie, it was just wonderful, just perfect." Even Teddy's voice seemed to be catching in his throat as well, and he choked out his words hoarsely. "If we made any mistakes, they were small ones. Maybe we shouldn't have mentioned Abergail's tits, eh Jamie? That made her yell so loud she didn't hear what I wanted her to do with her cunt. Boy, I'd like to have seen that!"

"Yeah, me too," Jamie said, but without too much enthusiasm. He was still not sure he shared his friend's attraction for cunts. Tits were great, but cunts still scared him. And besides, he thought, Miss Livingstone's didn't look all that much different from Barbara's, or the ones in the magazines, which, to him, all looked pretty much the same too. But he guessed that someday, when he was older, he would understand why cunts so fascinated other boys and men—and Teddy. "But otherwise things still went great, didn't they? Did you see Abergail's face when She came in, that frigging Abergail?"

"Yes," Teddy said. "Too bad we couldn't have figured out a way to get them both naked, eh, Jamie? Miss Livingstone's big tits and her hairy thing, and stupid, titless little Abergail —I bet she doesn't have any hair down there at all yet."

"But I don't either," Jamie said, suddenly ashamed of his immaturity,

"Oh, don't worry, Jamie, you'll have hair down there soon just like Tom does, and then we'll be able to do more than just look, won't we?"

Happiness returned to Jamie's face, and he imagined what he'd do when he got bigger. "Yeah," he said, "then we'll have some real adventures!" Although he wasn't at all clear just what they would be.

Suddenly he realized there were people downstairs, and for a panicky moment he thought Tom and Barbara had returned. The voices wafting up through the floorboards of his bedroom were definitely those of a man and a woman. Then he remembered. Sandy and that friend of hers, Allan, had gone out together earlier, Jamie hadn't expected her to bring him home, though, not to this home, to *his* home, to their home—his and Sandy's. And he knew it was late. It had been around eleven o'clock when he and Teddy had slipped out of the hedges surrounding Miss Livingstone's backyard, so it must be at least midnight now. Ever so quietly he changed into his pajamas and crawled into bed, with Teddy beside him.

When Sandy came in to check on him, all she'd find was a small blond boy fast asleep with an angel's smile on his face. He heard her climb the stairs, and he counted her steps as she came down the hall. The door opened soundlessly, and the muted light of the hall threw a narrow beam across the bed, illuminating his face. "Jamie?" The voice was just above a whisper. "Are you asleep?"

"Unnh," Jamie replied, doing what he felt was a pretty good impression of a sleeping person changing position slightly in bed. Her closeness to him caused his penis to grow erect again, and he expected her to come closer, to stand over him, maybe even to adjust the sheet, but she disappointed him. The door was closed as quietly as it had been opened, and the footsteps disappeared down the hall. Jamie's eyes snapped open. His mind was racing so fast it was beginning to stumble. "I'm going to go to her and do it tonight, Teddy, tonight!" he whispered.

"Yes, Jamie," the bear said softly, "this is the night for you to do it all right."

"Sleeping like a log," she told Allan. "Looking as pure and innocent as a baby."

"So," he said, "we should be okay then."

Sandy hesitated. In the car it had seemed like a good idea. Her tremendous relief that Allan was going to talk to Jamie, to take the terrible pressure off of her, had translated itself into sexual longing and her playfulness while Allan had tried to drive had excited them both. Now, however, she wasn't so sure; her sense of responsibility was beginning to raise its ugly head.

Sensing this, Allan had begun to marshal his arguments,

and while he tried to handle reluctance lightly, the edge on his voice left little doubt that he had every intention of seeing the matter through to its joyful conclusion. "Look," he said, "you just made me walk six blocks because you were so goddamned worried about the neighbors, you didn't want my car anywhere near the house. And you made me promise, on my Scout's honor that I wouldn't fall asleep right after— which I didn't—and—"

"Oh, you did *so*, Allan!"

"Well, maybe once or twice. Anyway, if the kid's dead to the world, who's to know—providing of course you can keep those orgasmic wailings of yours to a minimum."

She laughed and punched him on the arm. "Maybe I won't even come at all, Robert Redford. You're not all that great in the sack, you know."

"By their deeds shall you know them," he laughed back. "If you're still saying that half an hour from now I'll enter the seminary first thing in the morning. But if you happen to change your mind, I have some other filthy and disgusting ideas that need implementing."

They slipped off their sneakers and climbed the stairs hand in hand: Sandy motioned Allan to her room, then pointed to herself and then to Jamie's closed door. He nodded and, for the moment, they parted.

"Still fast asleep," she said, closing the door.

"Good," Allan replied.

He was already stripped down to his jockey shorts and fingering the waistband. She could see from the bulge that he was hall-erect and climbing, and she felt the electricity running through her. In seconds she was naked herself, the curves of her good young body glistening in the streetlight that filtered through the open window.

"Allan," she whispered throatily, and she crawled under the sheet beside him. "Take a long time please. Make it last a long time."

Then his mouth was on hers, his tongue flicking and caressing, and she shuddered happily. The last of the guilty, distressing thoughts of Jamie melted, then evaporated, and the only world she knew was the one inside her body.

CHAPTER SEVENTEEN

JAMIE GAVE himself about fifteen minutes after Sandy's second visit to his doorway, then slipped out of bed, pulled off his pajamas and drifted soundlessly across the braided rug to the door. He gave Teddy a little wave before stepping out, naked, into the hallway. Hugging the wall and trying to bring his breathing under control, he arrived at Sandy's closed door. But when he started to reach for the knob, the noise stopped him. The moaning sound. Was she sick? Was she hurt? He almost asked, but then some knowledge from somewhere told him to be quiet. So he waited a few moments longer.

The moaning continued, and it seemed to be getting faster, but not louder. Then he heard another sound, a deep groaning "Sandy, Oh Sandy!" sound that froze him to the spot. *He* was in there: Allan! The one that was supposed to be "just, a friend!" They were doing it! Sandy and… and that man! Jamie's mind began to reel, and hot tears began to run down his face. He thought he was going to be sick. Not really sure how he was doing it, he staggered back to his room.

And there was Teddy, black button eyes full of knowing and sympathy, sitting on the pillow. Despite what was happening to him, Jamie shut the door. Then he lurched to the bed and fell on it, his body wracked with silent sobbing, his fists pounding at the bedclothes, his legs kicking at empty air. After uncounted minutes, the spasms stopped. And uncounted minutes after that, he was able to look up into Teddy's eyes.

"They're... they're... oh, Teddy, they're..."

"I know," Teddy said, not unkindly.

"I thought she loved me. She said she did. She said he was just a friend. I..." Something inside him was pushing away the tears, the pain, the confusion. He felt himself becoming calm, and somehow terribly aware of everything around him. Teddy, the bed, the desk. Even his own hands, as he held them before his face, took on a new appearance, all suffused with silver light.

In a few more seconds his breathing was regular and his eyes were dry, and that strange glow had faded a bit—although it was still there, like a halo. He sat up on the bed and crossed his legs. His hands were in his lap. Slowly he turned and looked at himself in the dresser mirror and yes, even his reflection had that light around it. He stopped and looked more closely. *Funny*, he thought, *I never knew I looked like that*. He got up and went to the mirror, peering closely. *Is that really my face?*

"They'll have to be punished," Teddy said.

Jamie turned slowly, and a strange, far-off little smile crossed his lips, though his blue eyes were icy and hard.

"Yes," he said slowly, "they'll have to be punished."

He realized—was able to realize, despite everything—that while he had spoken, the voice was not his. It was Teddy's, or very much like Teddy's. Something was happening here, but he didn't understand what. All he did know was that it didn't scare him the way it probably should have. He looked in the mirror to check, once again, that he was still Jamie Benjamin, aged twelve. Yes, yes he was. And what's more, he liked the new smile too.

"I'll kill them now," he said in a manner no different than if he had said, "I have to go to the bathroom."

"Careful, Jamie," Teddy said. "We have to be very careful. Now think, Jamie. If you try to kill them now, you might fail. He's big, that Allan, and Sandy's young and strong."

Jamie nodded, but his eyes showed he was not fully convinced. "Yes," he said finally, "we have to plan, don't we? Like we did for Miss Livingstone."

"That's right, Jamie. Just like that. And we know a very good way, don't we?"

Jamie had to think for a few seconds, but Teddy didn't prompt him. "Yes," he said, the strange smile growing, we really do, don't we?"

"But first, Jamie, there are two things."

"Yes, Teddy," he said, lying down on the bed once again so that their faces were no more than a foot apart, "what are they?"

"First, I'd like to suggest that we still make all our plans together, like we did for Miss Livingstone. I do have a certain amount of experience in these things."

Jamie nodded.

"And second, you really have to watch your voice. Right now you sound too much like me, like the voice on the tape."

Jamie's smile broadened even further. "Great, Teddy, just great!" Then, "How was that, partner?"

"Perfect, Jamie. Just perfect."

OH CHRIST, Allan berated himself, *I've done it again*. Even before his vision was clear enough to read the watch he'd fumbled off the night table beside him, he knew, from the intensity of the sunlight in the room, that it was late—after eight, maybe closer to nine. He took no consolation from the fact that Sandy was still sleeping contentedly beside him. He'd promised not to fall asleep, and he had done it anyway, they'd fallen asleep together. But his immediate problem was not working up an apology or an apology or an explanation or even an escape attempt; he had to pee something fierce. And the kid, Jamie, just had to be up by now. Yes, Allan's watch confirmed, it was just a few minutes shy of nine o'clock. Gritting his teeth against the pain and strain of his overloaded bladder, he listened for sounds of activity in the house. Although he wasn't quite oriented in this strange bed in this strange room in this strange home, he guessed the noises were coming from the kitchen. Yes, the clack of crockery on crockery was unmistakable.

The kid was up and, apparently, he was making breakfast.

He slid out of bed, leaving Sandy blissfully undisturbed. If he was going to get shit—and he was—he preferred it on an empty bladder and, preferably, after at least two cups of coffee. He pulled on his underwear, retrieved the rest of his clothes from the floor, where he'd shucked them the night before, and left the room on tiptoes, pulling the door closed behind him. He listened briefly, then, satisfied that Sandy's breathing was unchanged, he searched out and found the bathroom.

He emerged a few minutes later fully dressed, much relieved, and with enough of a plan to buoy up his spirits at least slightly. Sometimes the direct approach was best, and he could only hope that this was one of those times.

"Hi, Jamie," he said, trying his best to sound offhanded and casual as he walked into the kitchen. "You couldn't spare a cup of coffee, could you?"

"Hi, Allan," the boy said. Either the kid was a great actor, or he was happy to see him—and not the least bit surprised by his being there. Given what he knew about Jamie—Sandy's perceptions—the second choice did not make one whole lot of sense. For that reason, it troubled him. But maybe, just maybe, Sandy had been exaggerating a little, as she did, he reflected, from time to time. Or maybe Jamie was just different with men, since there were no sexual tensions. *Yeah*, Allan thought, *that's possible. But isn't he going to ask me what I'm doing here?*

He stared with growing relief as the boy took a flowered mug from the set of six that hung under the counter beside the sink, unplugged the percolator, and poured the steaming coffee. "Cream and sugar?" he asked politely.

"No thanks." Allan managed. "Black is fine. It… uh… smells too good to dilute."

"Thank you, Allan," Jamie beamed. "Do you want some breakfast?"

"Uh… no thanks." *What the hell was this? What do you mean, Dressen? Why do you have to be so goddamned suspicious? The kid's being nice—no, more than nice and you're looking at him like he's some new lab rat. For Christ's sake, give him a break. Do you know what you're doing? You're committing the unpardonable yourself, sin of transference, and you ought to be ashamed of yourself.*

He sat down, lifted the mug, and took a little sip. "Great coffee," he said. Jamie shrugged and smiled shyly.

"I guess," Allan began, discovering that the little speech he'd prepared had been suddenly forgotten, "that, uh… you know I stayed here last night. I… we… I fell asleep. I'd been driving all day, or working, and I guess it just got to me. I must have passed out. I… hope you don't mind, Jamie. I hope that you won't have to tell your parents and get Sandy in trouble. I mean, God knows, I'm in enough trouble with her right now"

Jamie listened attentively to the explanation, and his bemused expression (or would have passed for bemused in an adult) never changed.

"Oh, don't worry, Allan," he replied very earnestly, "I

wouldn't think of getting Sandy in trouble. Or you, either. We're friends, aren't we? Sandy and I have lots of secrets that nobody else knows; we have lots of secrets." He stopped for a few seconds, and Allan could see that the boy was apparently wrestling with something. Then he came to a decision. "We have one secret that I'll tell you, Allan. I know I should ask her first, but I'm sure it'll be okay." He glanced at the ceiling. "Maybe we should wake her and ask her?"

No, Allan thought. But why not?

"She's pretty beat, Jamie. Maybe we should let her sleep. Why don't we go out for a walk or something, and we can talk and you can tell me your secret. Isn't there a donut shop or something in this neighborhood?"

"Sure. That's a great idea, Allan. But first I want to show you something—it's like part of my secret—if that's okay?"

"Fine by me." Allan said, downing the last of the coffee. "Now if I can just remember where I put my sneakers…"

While he was searching, Jamie washed and dried the cup and hung it back in its place. In his head he whistled his nameless, happy little Reverend Morley tune.

FOR SOME REASON, one which he had no intention of questioning, David had wakened in the best of all possible moods. And it had stayed with him. Even now, as he pushed the ancient hand mower along the boulevard in front of the house, it was still there. *What a great sound*, he smiled to himself. *Isn't it too bad that you hardly hear it any more, that people pollute the air with gas fumes or overload the electrical system instead of getting out there with the old hand mower and enjoying themselves? There must be whole generations of men now who have never felt this pleasure and never will.*

He was still congratulating himself on the discovery of this new truth when he saw the cruiser turn the corner and head in his direction. Helen was behind the wheel, he could see that, and he gave her a big smile and a wave. But she didn't wave back and she wasn't smiling. She stopped beside him, and her face said: there's trouble. David went over and crouched down, so that their faces were level. "I'm almost afraid to ask," he said.

"I'm sorry, David," she said. "I know you're off today, but something happened last night over at the Livingstone place, and..."

The Livingstone place? Margaret?

"Oh, Christ," he said, "is she okay? Was anybody hurt? What do you mean, Helen, what?"

"David? Oh, I'm sorry. I forgot. You've still... oh, never mind that." She told him rapidly what had taken place and what evidence there was to go on.

After she finished, David, who hadn't moved, demanded that she tell him again, but more slowly, step by ugly step. She did, and then explained, "She asked for you this morning, David. At first I thought it was because she didn't trust a woman cop, but then I remembered that you and she used to be friends, used to go together. I called a few minutes ago, but there was no answer—I guess you were out here cutting the grass and didn't hear the phone—so I took a chance and drove over."

"You didn't leave her alone?"

"Uh-uh. Fleischer is there with his fingerprint kit, and Cogan's out in the backyard, going over it square foot by square foot."

"Good," he said, standing and beginning his rapid stride toward the house. "You go ahead back. I'll get dressed and drive over myself."

Why the hell didn't she call me last night? Why the hell did she wait? What the fuck is going on in this town, anyway?

🐻

147

ALLAN TRIED to convince himself that it was a great morning for a stroll in the woods, though stroll was not exactly the right word. Following Jamie through thick, pathless underbrush, picking through patches of burrs, and trying to avoid impalement on thorns was more like running a gauntlet. But, Jamie kept telling him, the clearing was just a little ways ahead; and besides, how does a twenty-six-year-old man admit to himself that he can't do everything a twelve-year-old boy can?

He was in the midst of trying to come to terms with that when suddenly he found himself at the edge of a large, grassy field, about the size and shape of a football playing surface. But the surface, rather than being flat, was covered by rounded hummocks of varying sizes. Jamie, who had been five or ten feet in the lead throughout, broke into a run, but Allan didn't immediately follow suit. There was something about this place that he found, well, *foreboding*. Despite an eleven-day dry spell, the grass was lush and dark green. It was not even browned at the tips, and the air seemed to be filled with an unusual sweetness that he sort of recognized, but couldn't quite place.

Jamie had stopped and was waving at him with one hand, pointing with the other hand toward one particular mound, the largest in the field, Allan estimated, which was about thirty yards or so away. "There it is, Allan," he shouted. "Come on, I'll show you."

Ah, Allen thought, *the moment of truth. Now how do I handle it?*

He walked as slowly as he could toward Jamie, who was now at the side of the mound, leaning over it and speaking words that Allan could not quite make out from the distance. By the time they were side by side he still had no answer to his fundamental question: how do I handle it? The hole was a rough circle, he noted, about three feet in diameter.

"Down there," Jamie said, pointing. "That's where my friends are. The trogs."

"Jamie, I—"

"No, Allan, you can't see from there. You have to get closer."

Allan tested the footing, and, with some reluctance, took a step closer. All he could see is blackness. *Well, what did you expect to see, Dressen, King Kong?*

"I'm sorry, Jamie," he said, "but I'm afraid I can't see a thing." He hoped the boy wouldn't take it too badly, that it wouldn't screw him up to have one of his fantasies blown away.

"Don't worry, Allan," Jamie said amiably. "It takes a few minutes to get used to the dark. Besides, you're not close enough. You sort of have to lean over the hole." He dropped on his stomach and edged forward to demonstrate. "Don't be afraid, it's safe. I do it a lot." He stood and came around to Allan's side.

"Just do what I did," he said. "I'll hold your feet so there's no way you can fall. Okay?"

Allan did what he'd seen Jamie do. Jamie held his feet. Yes, there was a little light down there, but all it illuminated was dirt—dirt and nothing else. When he figured he'd done his part, he lifted his head and turned it toward Jamie. "I'm sorry, Jamie, but—"

Jamie yanked up violently on his feet. And Allan screamed, he slid, he grabbed for a hold—anything—and there was nothing to grab. Instinctively he turned over in midair and prepared to take the shock with his legs. The left leg twisted under the right and broke with a sickening tearing of muscle and flesh, and then the rest of him struck down, punching the air out of his lungs. He lay there on his back, the shattered leg bent crazily underneath him, staring up at the circle of light and fighting for even the tiniest of breaths. No pain yet, thank God. But soon. *Oh my God! Oh Christ! Oh no!*

"Jamie!" he rasped. "Jamie, for God's sake, help me! Get help! Get Sandy, Far, far above, the silhouette of a familiar head, the blond hair like a thin, bright halo, appeared.

"Jamie!"

"Good-bye, Allan," the silhouette said happily. And then it was gone.

He reached underneath, as best he could, to assess the damage to his leg. Oh Christ, he felt the mud that he knew had been mixed from his own blood. His probing fingers found the sharp, broken end of his shinbone under the denim of his jeans. He pulled the hand away instantly in fear and disgust, and he realized that, one way or another, he was going to die down here.

Then he heard sounds, far off, and no, he couldn't be sure if his mind was playing grotesque tricks. The sounds came closer, and he knew he had to be hallucinating. After all, what would a bunch of pigs be doing down here in this hole?

CHAPTER EIGHTEEN

SANDY DRIFTED SLOWLY, pleasantly into wakefulness. What a grand, wonderful day it must be, she mused, stretching like a cat in the sun, a little reluctant to open her eyes just yet in case the world wasn't quite as perfect and beautiful as she imagined. *Thank you Allan Dressen, thank you for last night—and for being you.* The thought made her want to giggle, so she did. You're never too old to giggle, she assured herself.

She opened her eyes now, and considered the empty side of the bed, last seen containing the fantastic body of the man she decided, for this moment at least, that she loved. *Isn't he just magnificent?* she thought. *I wonder what time he left? For that matter, I wonder what time it is now?*

The clock said it was precisely 10:35, which should have sent her flying out of bed in shame for yet another dereliction of her duty to Jamie Benjamin. But not today. Instead she stepped lightly into the bright patch of sunlight that warmed the gleaming hardwood. Then she stretched again, lifting off her sheer nightie in the process and letting it drift through the sunbeams to the floor. She danced around the room, feeling as free as Isadora, until she found herself face to face with her reflection in the mirror. So she smiled, curtsied, and said, "Good morning, Ms. O'Reilly. It's good to have you back."

"Thank you, Ms. O'Reilly," the mirror said. "It's good to be back."

With that, the real Ms. O'Reilly slipped into her silk robe and danced off down the hall to the bathroom. But she didn't quite make it. The phone began ringing, and for just a half-second or so it startled her, because it was only the second time in nearly a week that it had rung. *How odd*, she thought. *How odd that nobody ever phones here, and how odd that you can almost forget that such things as telephones exist.* She danced past the bathroom and into the master bedroom, where a simple black dial phone sat clanging away on the desk.

"Hello," she said brightly. "The Benjamin residence. Sandy O'Reilly, at your service."

"Well," Barbara Benjamin replied, "you're certainly in a good mood. Things must be going all right."

Sandy answered before she thought about it, but later, when she did think about it, she satisfied herself that there was really no other response, anyway. "Wonderful, Mrs. Benjamin—sorry, Barbara—just great."

"So… Jamie hasn't given you any trouble?"

Trouble? Well, not really. I mean, he really hasn't, has he?

"Oh no. We're getting along just fine. But how about you two?" *Let's get off the subject.* "How's the house hunting going?"

"That's why we called," Barbara said. "We've found his great place, just a few miles outside the city. It's an old farmhouse, all reconverted and modernized, of course, and authentically furnished. It has a pond and a barn, and twenty acres of land go with it. I can hardly wait to tell Jamie. Is he there?"

Oh shit, Sandy thought.

"Sandy?"

Oh, what the hell, it's just a little lie, "No, I'm afraid he's not. He took off about eight o'clock or so. Said he had something important to do." She was on the verge of saying she didn't know where he got his energy, but she realized that might be laying it on a bit thick. Barbara then said they'd be back on Tuesday, the only things left to do were to make arrangements with the bank in Seattle for the transfer of the down payment from Jericho and to sign the mortgage papers.

"Do you want me to tell him you called," Sandy asked, "or do you want to surprise him?"

"Oh, tell him," Barbara said. "Maybe he'll get used to the idea all that much faster."

Sandy hung up and began checking the house for Jamie, stopping to make his bed and pick up his yesterday's clothes along the way. *Well,* she said to herself finally, *at least he didn't make a liar out of me.*

She went back upstairs to the bathroom, decided against a shower—her breasts were still a bit too tender from last night to handle the hard spray—and selected a long, soft cotton peasant dress as her wardrobe for the day. She started to put on a bra, then said to hell with it. And to hell with panties, too.

SHE AND JAMIE arrived in the kitchen almost simultaneously. Sandy was carrying dirty laundry, en route to the basement, and he had a jarful of bugs in his hand, obviously headed in the same direction. "Hi," he said cheerily, "did you have a good sleep?"

"You bet I did," feeling very much in tune with his mood of the moment. "And you?"

"Great. Just great. But I had to get up because I had to find some bugs and stuff for my toads and snakes. I was real quiet. I didn't want to wake you."

"Thank you, Jamie," she said. "Listen, if you're going down to the basement, would you drop this in the laundry hamper for me. Then, after you've fed your pets, come on back up quick, because I've got some wonderful news for you."

He took the bundle and brushed her hand—deliberately, she knew; but today she didn't really mind. After he had disappeared down the stairs, she crossed to the opposite counter, where the percolator stood. *That's funny,* she thought, *it's almost full of coffee.* She smelled it and sort of thought it seemed fresh. She was almost sure she'd cleaned it yesterday. *Oh well,* she concluded, *I guess I couldn't have.*

DAVID STALKED around Margaret Livingstone's bedroom in impatient little circles while Margaret, slumped in a big, overstuffed easy chair, stared blankly and lit a series of cigarettes. After a couple of drags of each one she'd hold it out in disgust, make a sour face, and jam it out. Then, after a few minutes, she'd light another and repeat the process.

Sergeant Norm Fleischer, almost a little too small and a little too scholarly-looking to be taken for a cop, came into the room carrying three baggies, one with the note, one with the envelope, and one with the tape cassette.

"Well?" David said, calling a momentary halt to his pacing. Margaret crushed another cigarette and glanced up with what David thought was little more than mild curiosity.

"Not a thing," Fleischer said, pushing his glasses back up his nose where they belonged but rarely stayed. "Not even a partial. And, needless to say, the tape and the stationery are as common as the proverbial table salt—"

"But you're going to run a check, aren't you?" David interrupted. "The stationery shops, the supply houses?"

Fleischer looked from him to Margaret and back to him. As always, the sergeant's face was expressionless, "No,

David," he said evenly, "I'm not. We both know how bloody useless that is." Then, to Margaret, "Ms. Livingstone, I know how terrible this has been for you, how degrading. And I know how much it's upset your niece. And I'm sorry. But the truth is—and David will confirm this, when he calms down a bit—that the chances of finding this guy are just about nonexistent. He hasn't done it before, not that we know of, anyway, so we don't even have a pattern to go on. And he doesn't appear to have made any mistakes. And—no offense —but neither you or your niece has been able to help us much—"

David interrupted again. "Margaret," he said, crouching in front of her so she had to look him in the face if not in the eye, "are you sure you can't think of anyone? Somebody at the library who looked at you funny? A stranger hanging around there, maybe? Has Abergail ever had bad men stopping her on the street? ? Any strange cars driving slowly past the house? Anything?"

She looked at Fleischer, whose patience seemed to be endless, and then down at her own hands. But not at David. "There's only one person in this town who... who really bothers me, scares me. But I won't even tell you his name, because... because he couldn't have done it."

David put his hands on her shoulders and squeezed, harder than he'd meant to. "Who? Tell us, Margaret. How do you know he didn't do it?"

"Because," she said, looking him in the eye for the first time that morning, "he's only twelve years old."

TEDDY WAS VERY PLEASED. "You did good, Jamie, you really did good. And Allan was still alive when you left him, eh, and conscious? Very good. Tell me though, Jamie, honestly, do you feel sorry at all, do you feel even a little bit guilty?"

Jamie smiled and shook his head.

"Very good," Teddy repeated. "Now, do you think you'd like to do it again?" Jamie looked puzzled. Did Teddy mean to Sandy? No, no way. They had agreed on that. Sandy was the girl he loved, really loved, and now, with that Allan asshole out of the way, he'd have her.

"Oh no, Jamie," Teddy laughed. "I don't mean her. I mean the others, all the people in this town who have shit on you, fucked you over, for the last year. Let's see, there's Abergail, of course. And Freddy and lemon-tits Christina, and that frigging Miss Oliphant. Anybody else?"

Jamie thought for a moment, then shook his head. "There's a lot of people who deserve it, a lot of people I'd like to get even with, but there might not be time."

"Not time?" Teddy asked.

"Oh, I forgot to tell you, Teddy. Barbara called and we're probably going to be leaving for Seattle before next Saturday. And they're coming back here on Tuesday, so we'll really have to work fast."

"Yes," Teddy said, quite seriously, "we'd better draw up a schedule."

SANDY'S glorious feelings of that morning, about herself and Allan and life in general, were by late afternoon in imminent danger of collapse. The son of a bitch hadn't come back, and he hadn't phoned, and three calls to his apartment had resulted in precisely zero. Part of her wanted to kick his ass the moment he set foot again inside the door; but another part—an ever-growing one—was worried. It was simply not like him to do this. When Allan promised to do something, he delivered; or he had a very good reason for not delivering.

Her mother, had she been there, would have been urging Sandy to call the police and the hospitals, but her father, who was not the worrying kind, would have been drawling, "Oh, for Christ's sake, Marge."

Sandy had decided, a long time ago, that she was more like her father than her mother, whether that happened to be objectively true or not. No, dammit, it was much too soon to call the cops or anybody else, not today and maybe not even tomorrow. Allan would turn up, and when he did he better damn well have a good explanation.

She refocused her irritation on Jamie. It was nearly suppertime, and they had made a deal: she'd make the hamburgers if he went to the store for the meat. But he hadn't gone out, in fact, he hadn't come downstairs. She was tempted, really tempted, to go up there and give him her Number One lecture on responsibility, but then she stopped herself. *What you're doing, Sandy O'Reilly, is blaming the boy because Allan screwed up and got you all frustrated. Leave the kid alone.* She went to her purse, dug out her wallet, and stuck it in the big pocket of the peasant dress. Anyway, the walk would probably do her good, work off a little tension.

Sol Fruitman studied Sandy from the moment of her entry into the store until she was at his counter, asking for a pound of his best ground round. Normally she didn't mind being stared at—she knew she was young and pretty—but the five-minute walk had done nothing for the anger and worry she still felt over Allan's disappearance, and only returned a "good afternoon" because he had said it first and she'd been brought up to be polite. But Sol Fruitman, she quickly discovered, was a very perceptive man.

"Young lady," he said, so kindly that her momentary defensive shell just flaked away, "I know you are thinking that this dirty old man is staring at you and making up ideas in his head." She blushed. He noted it with a smile and continued his explanation. "It's not that, although you are a very pretty girl. It is just that—if I am wrong, forgive me—this is your first time in my store?"

"Yes," she said, "I'm not from around here. I'm just staying at the Benjamin place for a little while, sort of looking after Jamie?"

His left eyebrow rose, and he peered down at her a little more intently. "Excuse me for asking, Miss... uh..."

"O'Reilly. Sandra O'Reilly. Sandy. Oh, I'm sorry, I didn't mean to interrupt."

He waved it away. "No, I was just going to ask if you had already eaten all that hamburger young Jamie bought here yesterday? Four pounds, I believe it was."

All *what* hamburger? her face said.

"Oh," Fruitman said, "perhaps I shouldn't have mentioned it. The boy said it was for a barbecue, but perhaps it was with his friends, eh? That must be it. Of course. That's just what he said. You must excuse me, Miss O'Reilly, but I am no longer a young man. Sometimes, my mind goes, eh?"

Sandy wasn't listening, hadn't been since the words "four pounds." Jamie didn't bring home four pounds of hamburger. He didn't bring home *any* hamburger. She wouldn't have sent him for hamburger in the first place and certainly not four pounds of it. What else had this Mr. Fruitman said? For Jamie's "friends." Jamie had no friends, except... except... oh, shit, those stupid imaginary trolls or trogs or whatever he called them! Christ, had his fantasy gone that far?

"Is there something wrong, Miss O'Reilly?"

"I beg your pardon? Oh, I'm sorry, I just started thinking about something. No, he didn't tell me, but I guess I'd better take the ground round anyway. For all we know," she tried to salvage the situation with a joke, "he's feeding half the stray dogs in Jericho. He's... uh... quite a boy, our Jamie."

"Quite a boy," Sol Fruitman agreed, wrapping the meat carefully and tying it with a string.

On the way home, Sandy made a decision: she would not ask Jamie about the hamburger; she would not ask Jamie about anything else, if she could help it. She was sick of him, sick of his infantile sexual advances and sick of that cloying cheerful mood he'd been in for the last few days. Tuesday afternoon couldn't come soon enough.

TWENTY FEET BELOW THE EARTH, beyond the sight of any human eye, beyond the range of any human ear, five shadowy figures shared the last of the kill. They ate carefully, and with no sense of urgency, although the filthy, matted fur of their chests and stomachs was wet with blood.

All that remained of Allan Dressen was bones, a few apparently unappetizing internal organs, and a gore-drenched head with sightless, terrified eyes staring madly toward the little circle of sky. One of the creatures jabbered, and immediately all five set down what they held and formed a hunched circle.

The same creature who had first spoken, jabbered again. One of the others replied, then a third. They rose, gathered up the chewed and broken pieces of Allan Dressen, and disappeared down the tunnels.

CHAPTER NINETEEN

JAMIE COULD SEE that Sandy was in one of her bad moods. She was banging stuff around in the kitchen and muttering little curses under her breath and answering his questions with terse yeses, nos, and I-don't-knows. He decided not to ask what the matter was. After nearly a week in close quarters with Sandy, he had come to accept the occasional anger in her, even though he didn't quite understand what made her that way. Besides, he told himself, if you really love somebody, you have to put up with that sometimes; that's what he guessed, anyway.

They ate their hamburgers and their lettuce-and-tomato salads in silence. She drank coffee and he drank milk. She had made no offer of her famous limeade, and he hadn't requested any. When they both finished she stood and, without a word, gathered up their plates and glasses and cutlery and put them into the dishwasher, Then she left the kitchen and went directly to her room, closing the door hard behind her. Which was all okay with Jamie, who had been a bit worried earlier in the day about what reason he was going to give her for going out that night. He could have said that he'd been invited to the masquerade party over at Billy Jameson's house, but he doubted if she'd believe him; she knew he was never invited to parties or anything like that. Teddy hadn't been able to come up with an excuse either. He'd just said to try playing it by ear; probably Sandy wouldn't even ask Jamie where he was going, anyway.

Jamie consulted the kitchen clock. It was only 7:45, which meant at least two more hours of waiting. He needed darkness for this "mission," as Teddy had called it, he was almost ready to knock lightly and ask if he could help. Poor, poor Sandy, how unhappy she seemed sometimes. As good as the costume they'd decided upon was, it would be much more effective after sundown.

On his way to his room—he thought Teddy might want to come down to the basement with him while he tried on his outfit—he detoured on tiptoes to Sandy's door. He could hear her breathing, but he was pretty sure she wasn't crying. She did sigh a couple of times though, and times. Still, that was okay, because soon he would make her feel better. That's what people did who loved one another; they made each other feel better.

THAT EVENING, Billy Jameson's mom and dad created a party that the graduating class of James K. Polk would remember for years. The huge backyard had been strung with Chinese lanterns, and the three punch bowls were real cut glass, as were the little cups. There was even a sixteen-by-sixteen-foot dance floor, borrowed from the local VFW, where Billy's dad was president. And the music was provided by a five-man local group called Broken Promise, which had developed a following among both the younger people, at high school dances, and their parents as well, when it played the Holiday Inn. And her, about eleven o'clock or so, the man from New York Famous Pizza would arrive with plenty for everybody.

It all made Jamie feel a little bit wistful. At school he had been quite aware of the whispered invitations going around and he couldn't help but notice the guilty expressions on Billy's face when Jamie would accidentally draw within hearing range, but Jamie was so used to not being asked, being included, that it hadn't bothered him that much at the time.

Now he stood well off to one side, in the most shadowy part of the yard, watching a bejeweled princess and a tattered hobo dancing awkwardly to some song he didn't recognize but guessed had something to do with disco.

A couple of fat kids, dressed as Tweedledum and Tweedledee, Jamie supposed, were laughing stupidly and hitting one another over the head with foam rubber baseball bats. A cowboy was running around trying to lasso a giggling harem girl.

Then, by the bowl with the red punch in it, Jamie saw the two people who were his reason for being there. Freddy was dressed like a pirate, with a black eye-patch and a leathery kind of vest and red satin trousers ballooning out of turned-down black vinyl boots.

Lemon-tits Christina was in a white sequined ballet costume, complete with satin slippers, and her face was heavy with bright red lipstick and dark green eye shadow. Jamie watched the cowboy race a little too close to them, and he saw Freddy draw his wooden sword and wave it menacingly, bringing the cowboy up short and forcing him to move away.

Freddy shouted something after him that Jamie could not quite hear, although it might have been "Avast!" and Christina giggled idiotically and sort of fell against Freddy's bare chest. Then they both giggled, and Freddy stole a quick kiss. Christina tried to pretend she was mad at him, but she ended up giggling all the more as she punched, just like a girl, at his arm.

Jamie lifted the rubber skull mask away from his face, letting some air in and some of the dribbling sweat out. This mask and hooded sheet costume wasn't the most sensible outfit for the first day of summer, but it hid him completely from head to foot. The plan would be sure to fail, he and Teddy had figured, if he were recognized, if some of the other kids were able to say that the last time they'd seen them, Freddy and Christina were leaving the party with Jamie Benjamin.

With fingers interlocked, the pirate and the ballerina were walking away from the tables now, toward the darkest part of the yard, the part where Jamie stood and observed. He let them pass and then in the spooky voice he had practiced—Teddy had said it was perfect—he called after them. *"Fred-dee Hoek-straaa."*

The buccaneer turned to confront the ghost, and the ballerina took a step closer to her boyfriend and wrapped herself around his arm. The girl looked a little scared, Jamie thought, but as usual Freddy looked ready for a fight.

"Shove off, ghost!" he snarled, "or I'll run ya through!"

Lemon-tits giggled again and looked up at her hero lovingly.

"I have a message for you," the ghost said, still in its mock voice of doom. Freddy lifted his eye-patch and studied the skull face more closely; but Jamie was certain that not even his eyes would give him away in this light.

"So what are you waiting for?" Freddy demanded. "We don't have all night."

Okay, Jamie thought, *here goes.* He reached under the folds of the sheet and produced the note. Freddy took it and twisted partly sideways, holding the paper up to catch the faint glow coming from the Chinese lanterns. He read it once, then crumpled it up and threw it to the ground.

"Okay," he said, a mean little smile flickering across his face, "where is the little shithead?"

Without speaking, Jamie reached down and retrieved the note, stuffed it back under the sheet into his jeans pocket, and began walking away. Freddy's hand was instantly on his shoulder, jerking him back and holding him on the spot.

"Where, I said!?" Freddy's face was red and twitching with malice. Jamie, behind his skull mask, smiled. Slowly he lifted his right arm, extended the hand and then his index finger.

"Fol-low me, Fred-dee Hoek-straa, fol-low me and meet your doom!" Then he pulled away and began to walk quickly through the yard, out onto the street and toward the nearest entrance to the woods, about ten minutes away, by his earlier calculations. He didn't have to look back. He knew they were following.

"Freddy," he heard Christina whisper, "where are we going? What did it say in that note, Freddy? Where is he taking us?"

"You won't believe this," Freddy replied, "but that little dink Jamie Benjamin wants to fight me. The note said he's waiting to kick the shit out of me. Oh boy, Chrissie, I can hardly wait!"

Jamie stood at the broken-fence entrance to Whately's Copse and waited until they were beside him. "In there," he pointed. Freddy looked puzzled, then a little scared. Christina looked a lot scared; she wanted to run, and she wanted Freddy to run with her. She was glancing back down the empty road and pulling a little let's-get-out-of-here pull on Freddy's arm. Jamie leaned against the broken fence and folded his arms. "Don't be afraid," he said, "I know this forest very well. Just follow me."

"Freddy," Christiana whimpered, "I don't want to go into Whately's Copse. Oh, Freddy, please, let's go back to the party!"

JAMIE WANTED to laugh at her, but he thought better of it. He wasn't sure he could disguise his laugh as well as he had his voice. The final move in the plan was just too close now to mess it up. He had begun to feel the tingling, the excitement of it all. His mouth was getting dry and he had to gulp a couple of times to clear his throat. Then, in a voice heavy with sarcasm, he said, "If you're afraid, Fred-dee Hoek-straaa, then run away with your little friend. I will tell Jamie that you couldn't come tonight."

"I'm not afraid of anything, pal," Freddy said, shoving Christina aside and lunging for Jamie.

Jamie dodged and jumped into the woods, back-peddled a few feet and then beckoned slowly. Freddy grabbed Christina's hand roughly and dragged her, still sniveling, behind him. With the ease born of months of practice, Jamie floated through the woods in front of them, close enough to be seen and followed, but far enough ahead to avoid Freddy.

When Jamie got to the clearing he waited until they were just a few feet away, then ran hard to the side of the largest hummock. There, in the dim light he waited. Freddy wasn't feeling all that pirate-bold anymore, Jamie could see, but he kept up his pursuit, Christina still in tow.

At that moment Jamie strolled around the hummock and stopped to face the other two children, who were now positioned with the unseen hole between themselves and Jamie. Then, slowly, Jamie pulled back the hood of his costume and peeled off the rubber mask. "Hello, Freddy," he said in his own little-boy Jamie voice.

"You son of a bitch!" Freddy—his anger restored—yanked himself away from Christina's clutching hand and leaped across the mound of earth, his left hand reaching for Jamie's throat, his right balled into a fist. Then, suddenly, he found himself sliding down the edge of the hole, his arms failing, his hands grabbing for something, anything, to stop the fall. The boy's long scream, full of primitive terror, was abruptly cut off by a thumping crunch. Jamie didn't try to look down, since it was too dark to see. Instead, he walked slowly around the mound to Christina, who was standing there frozen, with rigid hands held to her mouth and eyes horror glazed. She didn't move, didn't even seem to notice as Jamie walked around behind her.

He grabbed her blond frizz with his left hand and twisted. The pain of that snapped Christina out of her spell, and she tried to struggle away. But Jamie held her tight and forced the girl down to her knees. With his free hand, he slid down the zipper of her ballet costume, then flipped her on her back and stripped the clothes off her shoulders and over her arms. Getting rid of the rest was more difficult, because getting clothes off girls was, after all, very new to him. Before long, though, he managed to strip away all the girl's clothes: her ballet costume, her little cotton panties, and the nearly cupless bra. All the time Christina just wept softly with no fight in her at all.

When at last he had her fully naked, Jamie stared at her body in the moonlight. Christina was all white, except for the little dots of her nipples and the skimpy patch between her legs. She did not make Jamie very excited, this skinny, pale, weeping child. He thought of Miss Livingstone and he thought of Sandy, and he felt a stirring down there. But then he looked at Christina, and the stirring went away.

Jamie He heard her panicked whisper. "Please, Jamie. Don't do anything to me. Please?"

Jamie smiled a terrible smile, and when he spoke, he saw her swollen eyes grow wider and wider with fright. *Oh, he* realized, *I'm using that voice, the one Teddy said to be careful not to use around people. Well, it really doesn't matter now, does it?*

"You laughed at me, Christina. You laughed when Freddy beat me up, when he called me dirty names, when he made me run away. You thought it was funny, didn't you?" He stepped forward and stood over her, looking down into that helpless, terrified face, and enjoying the sensation of having her completely within his power.

Then he reached forward and grabbed her by the hair again, pulling her to her feet with a strength that he'd never felt before. Using his other hand to twist her arm behind her, he then forced her to the lip of the hole.

"There's your fucking Freddy," he growled, pushing her face over the side. "You can't see him, but he's there. And soon my friends will come—oh yes, Christina, I do have friends—and they'll take care of him. They eat meat, Christina, young tender meat."

He released her hair, lifted up hard on the arm, and she lurched forward, down into the blackness. Jamie could tell from the soft crunch that she had landed right on top of Freddy. Christina gave one last little cry, and then there was no sound in the hole, the clearing, or the forest. The silence was total, unbroken by not even a cricket's chirrup or the messages of night birds. Jamie stretched out on his stomach on the safe part of the lip and peered into the depths below. "Hey," he said in his Jamie voice, "come on out. I've brought you more food. Something special."

In a few moments he heard the grunting, at first far-off but then, in a minute or two, directly below him. The grunting had come to sound almost like words, and Jamie was starting to believe he almost knew what his friends were saying to one another. The next thing he heard was flesh ripped from bone. How he wished he could see that! But it was just too dark down there. Maybe tomorrow he'd stay and watch.

AT TWENTY MINUTES after midnight on Sunday, June 22, Mildred Wagoner phoned Beatrice Hoekstra to ask if Christina was there. "No. Christina's not, and neither is Freddy." Beatrice Hoekstra said, Beatrice woke her husband, Ernie, who'd fallen asleep in front of the TV, and Ernie staggered into his car and drove over to the Jameson's house.

A sleepy but pleased Richard and Glenda were just taking down the last of the Chinese lanterns, and a yawning Billy was feeding the last of the leftover pizza into the disposal. Their mood changed quickly when Ernie arrived, and for the next half hour, in separate cars, Ernie and Richard and Vince Wagoner, who'd just come off shift at the paper mill, slowly patrolled the streets of Jericho, looking for a boy dressed up like a pirate and a girl dressed up like a ballerina.

Shortly after one A.M., Annie Goring, who was on duty that night, picked up the phone to hear the frightened voice of Mildred Wagoner tell her that Christina had disappeared. Annie took down the description, then flipped on her microphone and alerted the four officers on cruiser patrol to watch for a Christina Wagoner, four feet eleven inches tall, caucasian, blond, aged twelve; and Fredric Hoekstra, five feet four inches, caucasian, brown hair, aged thirteen; last seen wearing a ballet costume and a pirate outfit respectively.

At two thirty A.M., after another nearly hysterical call from Mildred Wagoner, Annie picked up the phone and dialed Chief Torrey's number. He listened sleepily, then instructed her to call everybody in. He would be there in about ten minutes to supervise the search. Annie lit a cigarette and dragged deeply a couple of times before lifting the receiver again. The boys and girls were not going to like this.

Before the sun rose, every other child who had been at the party, every other child save two—Abergail Buhl and Jamie Benjamin—in the graduating class of James K. Polk, had been shaken awake by half-asleep, berobed parents, and brought into living rooms to be closely questioned by police officers. Not one of them remembered when Freddy and Christina had left the party. It was such a fun party and they'd all been having such a good time that they hadn't much noticed Freddy and Christina. A few recalled that the two weren't around when the pizza came, about eleven, but they hadn't thought too much about it because Freddy and Christina often just sort of went off alone together.

About six A.M., old Scotty Tumbrell, who was proud to think of himself as the official town drunk—a belief with which the police department and the other citizens fully agreed—woke from his usual stupor with a powerful hunger. He wandered out of the park and down an empty Main Street toward John & Jane's Diner to see what the garbage cans had to offer.

He started to reach into the first can, then yanked back his hand and blinked. Right on top, its sequins glinting in the slanted rays of the morning sunlight, was what looked like a wedding dress. Gingerly he lifted the strange garment out and held it up. He was still trying to figure out what the thing was when a car screeched up behind him, a door opened, and David Bentley's knife-edged voice said, "Freeze, mister!"

When Scotty turned, all he saw was the huge black hole of the gun muzzle. But before David could say, "Oh, relax, Scotty," now that he recognized the old guy, Scotty had passed out.

CHAPTER TWENTY

"Good morning, Miss Oliphant," Jamie said.

"Who's that?" Miss Oliphant snapped. She peered in the direction of the voice but could perceive only a gray shape.

He came closer, stood behind the wheelchair, and introduced himself. "It's me, Miss Oliphant, Jamie Benjamin." She stiffened. But Jamie's voice was soothing. "Please, Miss Oliphant, please don't be mad at me. I just wanted to talk to you for a while. I mean, we're moving, I mean my parents and I are going away for good, and I just wanted to apologize to you before I go. I know I was bad, that I said awful things to you, and I'm really sorry, honest I am."

She couldn't quite understand why the boy was trying to be nice, but she relaxed some anyway. She still wished, however, that Louise would come back. She knew now that she should have accepted Louise's invitation to come to church with her, instead of sitting alone and helpless outside in the park, but it just wasn't in Miss Oliphant's Baptist soul to cross the threshold of an Episcopalian church. It was too close to Papist for her liking.

"Well, Jamie Benjamin," she said, forcing herself to be at least civil with the boy, "I accept your apology."

"Oh thank you, Miss Oliphant," he replied happily. Then he reached down and eased Miss Oliphant out from under her shade tree and onto the wide macadam path that cut diagonally through the park. The path ended at the two-lane blacktop of the secondary highway that divided the built-up edge of Jericho from Whately's Copse and the farmland beyond.

"Jamie! What are you doing, boy?" The boy had given her no warning. He hadn't even asked if she wanted a ride; he had just started to push Miss Oliphant along. "Stop it this instant, do you hear me?" They were soon out of the park; and the road—because it was just a few minutes after nine on a quiet Sunday morning—was deserted. Miss Oliphant did not know this, of course, and she began to holler for help in her cracking old-lady's voice. But Jamie just kept pushing faster and faster down the road and across onto the gravel, then through long sun-dried grass and finally to the fence itself.

Miss Oliphant twisted in the chair, trying to fall forward. If she could just get out, she thought in increasing panic, perhaps this boy would be too weak to get her back in. But no, there was no chance. If he was going to harm her—and her mind was bursting with images of rape and murder and mutilation—he would not be stopped. Why, oh why, could nobody hear? Why didn't somebody come along? *Oh, Blessed Jesus, please save me!*

Then... salvation! She heard a car coming. They'd see, they'd hear, and she'd be saved. What Miss Oliphant couldn't know, however, in her world of dim sight, was that she and Jamie were already hidden from the road by brush and tall grass. And she would not be heard, either. Strong hands had her by the throat from behind, squeezing, and the most terrible evil voice she'd ever heard spoke a few inches from her ear.

"If you make one sound, you dried-up old cunt, I'll kill

you right here." There was no inflection in the voice, no anger. Just a flat statement that was so full of vicious threat that she wet herself in fear. The car passed and the grip on her throat was relinquished.

Then she was moving again, bumping and dragging over a floor of rotted leaves and soft rich black earth, her face and body and arms constantly lashed and cut open by low tree branches and high bushes. She was being hurled forward faster and faster, and all she could do was to cling tightly to the arms of the wheelchair and whimper long-neglected, half-remembered prayers for forgiveness and deliverance.

Then, she realized, the chair had stopped. She felt the full force of the warm June morning sun, and a soft breeze stirred her hair and caressed her scratched and torn skin. She sensed that Jamie—or whoever this monster was—had moved away from her, and she squinted, picking up movement to the right ahead of her. The boy seemed to be lying face down on a small hill, but she could tell no more than that. Then her other senses, improved by twenty years of functional blindness, came into play. She immediately wished they hadn't, that the superb hearing and sense of smell she'd developed in compensation for her blindness had gone with her sight.

She knew the smell. After more than fifty years, she remembered it, even remembered how sick it had made her the first time, how, after she'd left that abattoir in Springfield, Illinois, she'd rushed across the street and vomited behind the bushes until nothing was left to come up.

But she didn't know the sound, though she did know it was a noise she never ever wanted to hear again; the only image she could give that terrible sound was of a huge, hungry dog, ripping and chewing meat from a fresh bone. Her stomach, fueled only by two pieces of toast and a cup of tea that morning, began to roil and erupt, and her hands went instinctively to her mouth. She began to gag, and she felt the sour, hot liquid dribble on her hands and down her chin.

Then in her chest something exploded, and agony boded up into her shoulder, down her left arm, back up again into the chest, redoubling the pain every second. Heart attack. The stink and sound of ugly death faded, returned, worse than before but only briefly, and then was gone. She knew she was dying, and she was satisfied. Soon it would be bearable, soon she would be unconscious and she would never wake again. One more great spasm, and...

Jamie looked up from the hole, from watching his friends feed on the last of Freddy Hoekstra and Christina Wagoner, their "midnight snack," as he'd come to regard it. The old woman was gasping, her breath whistling in and out of her; her body arched forward, then threw itself back against the chair; then she slumped and was very, very still. The boy stood up and went over to her. He lifted off the dark glasses and looked inquisitively into the empty, rheumy, washed-out eyes. He replaced the glasses, leaned down, and put his ear against her chest and listened for a few seconds before straightening and stepping back. Then he went around behind the chair, shoved it forward until it was near the top of the hummock's slope, and tipped her out. Next he moved the chair away, lifted Miss Oliphant up onto the lip of the hole, and rolled her in.

"Look out below!" he yelled in his Jamie voice, realizing just as Miss Oliphant dropped from his sight that his five friends were still down there munching on Freddy and Christina. He was pleased to see when he looked a second or two later that his friends had managed to get out of the way in time. They were all looking up now, yellow eyes blinking; more than ever before, Jamie believed that they knew him and that they understood what he was doing for them.

The figures, while he watched with fascination, formed a tight little circle and began that grunting jabber of theirs;

then they broke off and looked up at him again. One of them
—the one Jamie had determined was the leader, although he
couldn't be sure because they looked so much alike—raised a
clawed hand and pointed at him, then back to its own,
bloodied mouth. Jamie thought it was smiling—its eyes had
seemed different, softer—but he wasn't sure about that,
either.

"Yes, yes!" he said, pointing at the partly visible corpses of
Freddy and Christina, their heads, like Allan's, apparently
unpalatable and therefore uneaten, and at the broken body of
Miss Oliphant, collapsed there facedown. "Oh yes, that's
right. Food!" He pointed to his own mouth and made
chewing sounds and movements with his teeth and face.

The yellow eyes seemed to grow excited, and there was
another short conference down below. Then they all looked
up at Jamie again, and the leader grunted "Furrd?"

"Oh yes," Jamie laughed, clapping his hands in a very little
boy gesture, "that's right! Food!"

"Furrd," the creature said.

By ELEVEN A.M., Chief Becker Torrey and his officers had
just about reached a consensus. They were agreed that
Freddy Hoekstra and Christina Wagoner must have been
abducted after they had left the party at the Jameson place.
They must have accepted a ride in a car with a man (or men),
who must have taken them out of Jericho entirely. With
nothing more to go on than Christina's ballet costume and
cotton panties that Scotty Tumbrell had found stuffed in a
garbage can, kidnapping seemed the most likely guess. Radio
bulletins, which had been playing since about eight-thirty
that morning, had produced not one helpful call.

David slipped off the desk top he'd been occupying
silently throughout the briefing and wandered over to the

coffee maker. He poured a half-mugful, sipped it, and made a disgusted face. He had not been willing to go along with the consensus, but at the same time he had not felt ready to explain just why.

From the moment he'd drawn down on poor Scotty Tumbrell that morning and whisked up the ballet outfit where Scotty dropped it, his mind had kept wanting to make a connection between this disappearance and that of the Reverend Morley and—and this was the truly tenuous part— the horror that Margaret Livingstone had been subjected to. The trouble was there was no connection other than proximity in time. In his imagination—where it would have to most certainly stay for now—he saw a faceless, nameless, almost formless maniac, loose in this town, in their midst. And he believed that in some unfathomable way a nightmare had begun in Jericho that would not end that day. And yet... and yet... why, in his mind, did every scenario take him back to that clearing in Whately's Copse, to the mound, to the hole where he'd felt such evil?

"David," he heard Torrey's voice through his distant musings, "do you have anything to say?"

David looked in the direction of the voice and brought the broad black face into proper focus.

"No," he said after a few moments of reflection, "I don't."

After the officers split up, with each assigned to a predetermined point to meet and command search teams, David climbed into his Camaro and sped away on a short personal mission. A few minutes later he was leaning over the hole, his sinuses already plugged and his sense of smell almost fully blunted, shining his flashlight down into the blackness. Everything was as he'd left it, he thought. Then, from down there, but from far, far away, came a faint, rustling sound. He listened intently, stretching dangerously over the edge, and he was almost sure he heard it again. Then, nothing, only undisturbed silence.

He was still moving carefully through the woods, back to his car, when he heard the squawking of the police radio. Annie Goring, on double shift, was calling out his personal code. With his arms up to protect his face, he plunged through the remaining fifteen or twenty feet of growth, hopped the wooden fence, and grabbed the receiver through the window. "Yeah, Annie, what is it?"

"David," she said, "I'm afraid we have another one for you."

"What?"

"A Miss Oliphant. Late seventies, blind. In a wheelchair. Lady who looks after her came out of St. Bartholomew's church approximately nine fifty A.M. today. Not in park across street, where left. Not at home."

"Holy shit!" David replied, his button down.

"Watch the language, boy." It was Torrey's voice this time.

"Sorry, Beck. What do you want me to do?"

"Come back in here first and calm down this Louise Persons woman for me and see what you can get out of her. I'll put somebody else at your search point... if I can find somebody."

David had already screeched the Camaro into a U-turn and was halfway back to the station before Torrey had finished talking. "On the way," he reported. A long-forgotten snatch of poetry was running through his mind, and it just wouldn't leave him.

"By the pricking of our thumbs," he muttered to himself, "something wicked this way comes."

SANDY, still in a robe with her curly hair untended, wandered into the kitchen about one thirty on Sunday afternoon; absently she rummaged through cupboard after cupboard, spied a box of saltine crackers and guessed that maybe they'd do. She ate them at the counter, looking out the window into the hot, empty backyard.

For a fleeting moment she worried about where Jamie might be, and then she thought about phoning Allan's place one more futile time. *No, she let inertia decide, I just can't face the futility of it; I just can't stand the sound of that ringing telephone again just yet.* She shoved the last three uneaten crackers haphazardly back into the waxed paper sleeve, twisted the thing closed—or mostly closed—and returned it to the box, which she left sitting on the counter. She drank two glasses of water and returned wearily to her room.

A few minutes later there was a light knock on her door and she invited, without enthusiasm, Jamie to come in. He just stood in the doorway and asked with what seemed to be genuine concern, if she was sick. "Is there anything I can get you?" he continued.

"I may be getting summer flu or something like that," she lied—anything to get him away. "And no thanks, I really don't want anything. But if you like, you can get the chicken breasts out of the freezer, and we can have them for supper." Then Sandy remembered that she was there in that house to take care of Jamie and not the other way around, so she asked him how he was doing, was there anything he wanted or needed?

"Oh, no, thank you Sandy," he beamed. "Everything is just great."

She should have asked where he'd been last night and again this morning, but she didn't seem to care. Two more days and she'd be gone, out of this place and away from this weird little boy, whose presence increasingly made her want to get into a steaming hot bath and disinfect herself.

CHAPTER TWENTY-ONE

AND THEN IT was the morning of the next to last day of school. Jamie gobbled his scrambled eggs and sausages, and drained off the tumblerful of milk in three or four gulps. Sandy, in the same silk robe she'd worn all of the day before, chewed without either pleasure or interest on a piece of dry toast and let her coffee grow cold in front of her. Jamie guessed she was still sick with the flu, but he had other things to be concerned about.

Still chewing, he got up from the table, found a couple of textbooks he'd brought home the previous Friday and left unopened, and plunged out the back door, letting it slam. When he got to the sidewalk he slowed his pace and strolled toward the school the way he always did, head down, arms swinging lightly at his sides.

As he passed Christina's house, he sneaked a little glance. There was a black car in the driveway that he thought belonged to Dr. Gooderham, but there was nobody around outside and all the shades were drawn. Jamie thought about Christina's naked body, lying there in the clearing in the moonlight, but he couldn't hold the image in focus. It just drifted away from him and, try as he could to recapture the sensations of that wonderful Saturday night, he just couldn't do it. Then he saw Allan, staring up at him with those dead eyes, and that stayed a little longer, making him smile. And Miss Oliphant, that was good too.

He turned the corner and stopped. He had already determined the spot where he was unlikely to be seen from the street. If he crouched behind the big maple, he had a clear view of Abergail's house. If she did what she always did on school mornings, in a few minutes she'd come walking her bike along the side. Then in front of the house she'd wave one last time to Miss Livingstone, who'd be standing in the living room window, and ride away.

When she came around the corner, the one where he was lying in wait for her, she'd be out of Miss Livingstone's sight. Jamie reached into his shirt pocket and pulled out a bent, crumpled, dry old cigarette, the last of a pack he'd pilfered from Tom's drawer nearly six months before. Jamie had decided then to try smoking, but that hadn't much appeal to him. He lit the cigarette, choked out a few strangled coughs, and then puffed away amateurishly. Just a precaution, that's all. With all the people missing, maybe even a twelve-year-old kid might be questioned if he were caught sneaking around; and the cigarette, sure as heck, would explain the sneaking.

There she is! Funny, she didn't wave this time. Oh, Miss Livingstone is not at the window.

Here she comes. Get ready. Get set. Go!

"Abergail!"

She half-leaped, half-fell, landing hard on the boulevard as the bike skidded and spun down the sidewalk to a stop almost at Jamie's feet. If Abergail was stunned by her fall, she didn't show it, and she was halfway back to her feet by the time Jamie had the bicycle upright and was throwing his leg over the saddle.

"I'll kill you, you little bastard!" she gasped, fighting to retrieve the breath that had been knocked out of her by the shock of the fall.

Ah, Jamie thought, *just the way we planned it.*

He peddled away slowly enough to give her time to catch that lost breath and take off after him. He checked the rearview mirrors on this most wonderful of bicycles and adjusted his speed to keep her at a close, constant distance behind him. At the next corner he turned left, away from the route to school; and, after about thirty feet, he stopped to make sure she was still coming. He let her come closer, close enough so that he could see the fury in her little green eyes and hear the angry panting. Then he took off again, toward the old highway and what lay just a few hundred feet to the right on the other side.

A huge gravel truck was approaching from the opposite direction as he wheeled out. *If the driver sees us,* Jamie instantly realized, *he might remember and there might be trouble.* So he increased his speed, putting more distance than he really liked between himself and Abergail; as the truck passed, he gave the driver a big wave and a big smile, all natural and nice, and the driver returned it, plus a little honk on the horn. Then, beautifully, the road was empty.

He slowed again. Then, when he saw the break in the fence, he wheeled left over the gravel and grass and through the low brush to the gap. About ten feet into the woods he stopped and dismounted, leaning the bike against a tree. He unhooked the gleaming chrome bicycle pump, hefted it, and waited for Abergail to come crashing in.

Which she did, her eyes wild and her fists bunched.

He stepped from behind the tree and swung the pump as hard as he could at her face. It caught her nose right at the bridge, making a crack he could both hear and feel. Blood gushed from the mangled nose, and her eyes went wild and began to roll back in her head. She swayed, reached out blindly for support that was not there, and dropped heavily to the ground. Jamie stepped forward, the pump raised. After a few seconds, after he was sure that she would not be getting up for a while, he lowered the pump and smiled.

By the time Jamie'd dragged her to the hole, and laid her face downward over it, dripping blood into the soil below, Abergail had begun to stir a little, and to make little mewing noises. He stretched out beside her and, gripping her by the hair, turned her face toward his, so that their eyes were mere inches apart. He gave her his best Jamie smile this time and was quite pleased at the reaction, the hate and terror that were in her eyes.

"Well, Cruel Buhl," he said pleasantly, "don't you look nice today."

"Rotten disgusting filthy little bastard," she choked out, "lousy pervert." She spit in his face, a great pinkish bloody blob of it that struck him just below his left eye and ran down his cheek. Jamie did nothing more than wipe away at it with his free hand, examine it curiously, then rub it into her hair.

She tried to pull away, but he was having none of that.

He twisted his left hand more tightly in her hair, and slowly forced her head back to the point where the pain would block out any other thoughts, prevent any other movement.

"Oh no, Abergail," he said, his tone unchanged, his voice still a little boy's. "You don't want to leave. I have a real treat in store for you, something you'll remember for a long, long time." Then he turned his head away and shouted down into the hole, "Hi, it's Jamie. It's time for food."

MRS. LYNDE WAS NOT in the least curious about why Jamie had arrived in the classroom half an hour late. She didn't even bother to ask where he'd been. Out of a class of twenty-seven, there were eleven students—twelve now—that had showed up, and neither she nor they could find any good reason for being in school.

Freddy and Christina were still missing, and a lot of frightened parents had kept their kids at home. She didn't blame them a bit. It had been funny, walking to the school that morning. How silent the streets had been, how few children about; the town just seemed to be closing itself up.

After a few minutes she left her own musings and observed her few students, studying each face and trying to figure what was going through the brains behind them. Pretty much what was going through her own, she guessed: fear, uncertainty, confusion. Except for Jamie Benjamin. Didn't he know what had happened? Hadn't anybody told him? Didn't he listen to the radio? Just what in the hell was going on in his head what was so goddamned amusing?

"Mrs. Benjamin?"

"Ugh, no," Sandy said. "She's… they're away. I'm the baby-sitter." Like most people, Sandy didn't know how to talk with policemen, or, as in this case, policewomen.

And it was the first time in her life that one had actually come to the door. For a few seconds Sandy just stood there, arms hanging at her sides, terrible visions flitting in and out of her mind. Was it Allan? No, or the policewoman wouldn't have asked if she were Mrs. Benjamin, would she? *Oh God, it must be Jamie!*

"Is he all right?" she managed.

The woman looked confused and, Sandy noticed for the first time, very, very tired. Her uniform was wrinkled, and the short blond curls as messy as her own hair. There were spreading sweat stains under each armpit, and the hazel eyes seemed to be moving in and out of focus.

"I beg your pardon, Miss… Miss…"

"O'Reilly. Sandra O'Reilly." Then, "Jamie? Is he all right?"

Somehow, Helen McLachlan worked up a weary little smile. "Oh, yes," she said. "I just left him at the school. Yes, he's okay."

"Then what…?" *It had to be Allan! Oh, my God!*

"Two children—from Jamie's class, as a matter of fact—disappeared on Saturday night. And yesterday morning, an old woman named Oliphant also disappeared. And…"

As Helen talked, Sandy was motioning her into the house, into the cool of the darkened living room, and they both sat.

"I can't take long, Miss O'Reilly." Helen said, taking in as much of the room as she could. "We're doing a house-to-house search of the whole town, and I'd just like to take a quick look around and be on my way." She opened her notebook and checked something. "I've got thirty-four more on my list."

"You look awfully tired," Sandy said, fully recovered now from her near faint. "Can I get you some coffee or something?"

Helen shook her head unhappily. "No, I'm afraid I haven't got time for that. But thank you. And yeah, I am pretty beat. Been at this nonstop since early Sunday morning, like about two A.M. Oh well, like the man said, a policeman's lot is not a happy one."

"Gilbert and Sullivan," Sandy muttered.

"I beg your pardon," Helen said.

"Nothing, I…" She could feel her face getting red. What a stupid thing to say at a time like this! "I just… uh… remembered something. Anyway, come on, I'll show you the house. But I don't think it'll help you much. Jamie… uh, Jamie didn't have much to do with the kids in his class."

"So we discovered," Helen said, rising from the leather chair. "Well, okay, let's get it over with. It's just something we have to do, that's all."

Ten minutes later, Sandy was saying good-bye to the exhausted policewoman at the front door and wishing her luck, hoping that everything would turn out all right. She had thought about bringing up the business of Allan, how she hadn't seen him since Friday night, but she just felt so silly and unsure she let it lie.

This officer and the whole department had so much on their hands that it seemed terribly silly to lay something else on them. What if she did tell them and then, an hour or so later Allan came driving up as if nothing was wrong? No, she'd try his apartment a few more times first and then, if she hadn't heard from him by tomorrow, she'd call the police.

At one point she'd actually wondered if he *had* actually disappeared, been kidnapped or abducted or whatever the right word was, like the two kids and the old woman, but she just couldn't make it jibe. Allan was a big, powerful young man who had survived, with his fists and his wits, one of the toughest high schools in Toledo, Ohio. He was no kid, no old lady.

After Helen had gone, crossing the lawn to the house next door, Sandy experienced a flicker of fear that froze her belly for a few seconds.

Jamie? No, don't be ridiculous? How could a twelve-year-old boy be responsible? But Jamie did know all the missing people, Miss Oliphant and the two children, and... Allan. But he didn't know the old minister, did he? So? So, nothing. Leave the kid alone, for Godsakes.

She checked the kitchen clock. A few minutes past noon. In twenty-four more hours, Tom and Barbara Benjamin would be driving in from Madison and she'd be free.

ONCE AGAIN, David blessed his father's foresight. If the house had been two more minutes from the station, David was certain, he would never have made it in time. As it was, he had to make a decision whether he'd walk to the house or crawl on his hands and knees or just keel over in the front seat of the car, there in the driveway, and pass out.

He chose the first option, chuckling giddily to himself about how he couldn't disgrace the uniform—a uniform that at that very minute was dirty and sweaty and wrinkled almost beyond redemption. Besides, he longed for the air-conditioned bedroom, the cool sheets, a nice shower and a couple of glasses of milk to soothe the burning in his stomach. And he wanted to call Margaret one more time to see how she was doing.

God, Friday night had been so long ago. He also hoped that this time Abergail would be at school, so that she would not answer the phone in that cold, too mature voice of hers, and say that her aunt was "resting," and that if he had any messages, she would pass them along. Unless, of course, it was police business.

"No, it wasn't," he'd said.

"Fine," the child had replied, "then I will ask her to call you when she feels better."

The phone rang a dozen times, and David, despite himself, closed his eyes and began to doze. He didn't hear the receiver being picked up, but when it was dropped, striking something hard and probably wooden, he snapped momentarily back to attention. "Margaret? Margaret, is that you?'

"Hello. Hello." The voice was flat and soft and weak, like it was coming from a long way off, not physically, but emotionally. "Who's calling, please?"

"Margaret, it's David. David Bentley. Are you all right?"

"Oh, David. Yes, I'm fine, David," she continued serenely and tonelessly. "Just a little tired, that's all. I've been sleeping." He waited, the receiver growing heavier and heavier in his hand.

Finally he said, "Is there anything I can do, Margaret:

anything I can bring you? Have you seen the doctor again—since Saturday morning I mean? What does he say?"

After another silence, she replied, "The doctor? Oh yes, he gave me some pills. They make me want to sleep. Guess I'd better get up now, though. Uh, what time is it, David."

He checked his watch. "About three-fifteen," he said.

"Oh, then Abergail will be home soon. I'll just have another little nap and then I'll get up and make her something nice for supper. She's been awfully good, David."

"I know," he said, unable to think of anything to the contrary and not really trying to. "Well, take care of yourself. I'll try to drop around tomorrow."

"Yes, David, that would be very nice."

CHAPTER TWENTY-TWO

By THE TIME Jamie arrived home, Sandy had read and reread the newspaper and, out of a vague sense of obligation, was hauling out the vacuum cleaner as the first step toward presenting the Benjamins with a clean house on their return. The events of the past few days were, at least for the moment, not quite digested. All those missing people in such a short time with no clues whatsoever, was a fact she just couldn't fully acknowledge, let alone come to terms with.

At lunch, shortly after the policewoman had left, she'd asked Jamie questions about the Hoekstra boy and the Wagoner girl. What were they like, did he know them very well, that sort of thing. Jamie had given nothing answers, but he had seemed properly sober and reflective about it all.

When she mentioned Miss Oliphant, he had replied that sure, she'd been pretty mean to him and everything and had gotten his bicycle taken away, but he hoped she'd be okay anyway because she was old and blind and had to be in that wheelchair, and it probably wasn't really her fault that she was so mean. Sandy'd asked if he was scared, and he'd said that he was, maybe a little bit, but that with all the cops running around everywhere, he didn't think anything else was going to happen.

In some ways, that conversation had reassured her a little about Jamie; there was something certainly out of place in his attitude, and his concern for Miss Oliphant and the two kids seemed, at least on the surface, quite genuine. That made her feel a little better, and by doing the cleaning-up, she began to believe she might even finish this job on some kind of positive note. Which was better, healthier, than the attitude she'd started it with.

AFTER JAMIE GREETED her that afternoon, he went directly to his room. A few minutes later he came back down to the living room, where she was polishing the glass-topped end table, rummaged silently through the wicker magazine rack, selected a copy of something-or-other, greeted her again and went back upstairs.

"I don't know," Teddy said. "Isn't it taking a bit of a chance?"

"Don't worry," Jamie replied, not looking up from the page. He ran the X-acto knife along each line, searching for the letter combinations that would require the least cutting. He found an "ail" and neatly excised it, transferring it to the clean sheet of white paper on the desk beside him.

"Jamie," Teddy said, a touch of pleading in his voice now, "we've made it so far, but we can't get careless, not with only a few more days to go here. It's not worth it, Jamie."

The boy reached into his shirt pocket and pulled out a much-folded, scruffy-looking piece of paper. He opened it carefully and lifted out the contents, a couple of dozen red hairs still attached to a small, dried-bloody piece of human scalp. He held it up for Teddy to see and pointed excitedly. "This, Teddy, look at this! It's just too good to waste."

"Okay, Jamie," the bear sighed. "I guess it's all your show now anyway."

"Oh, Teddy, please don't talk that way." He put down the knife and went over to the bed; he lifted Teddy up and held him close, speaking soothingly and rocking a little from side to side on his feet. "It's okay, Teddy, don't be afraid, I'll..." Then he stopped and held the bear at arm's length, and a funny little grin crossed his face. "Why, Teddy," he said, almost derisively, "I know what your trouble is! It's Miss Livingstone, isn't it? You still love Miss Livingstone?"

Teddy didn't answer.

"Well, do you?" Jamie teased.

"No," Teddy said in a very small voice. "You just do what you have to do, okay? And if you need me, if you need my help some time, don't worry, I'll be here."

"I'm going to fuck Sandy tonight," Jamie said, out of nowhere.

Teddy's button eyes brightened a little. "Best of luck," he said.

THE HOUSEWORK COMBINED with everything else had just about exhausted her. Well, at least the downstairs was done, and she could do the rest in the morning when Jamie was at school. Besides, she had begun to smell herself, and she stank. She lifted her arm and sniffed tentatively, then made a disgusted face.

"Uggh," she muttered, "you better hope that Allan doesn't show up now." She put away the vacuum, the polishes, and the soft cloths, and dragged herself upstairs to the bathroom. She started the shower, adjusted for the temperature she preferred, and then peeled off the sticky T-shirt and bra. She started to unzip the fly of her jeans, then stopped and went over to the door. No, it was just her imagination. She pressed her ear against it for a few more seconds, then straightened, more reassured now. But, just as a precaution, she pushed in the little button in the middle of the doorknob and gave it a quarter turn.

She stepped out of her jeans, rolled down her panties, took one more look at the locked door and stepped into the hard, warm spray. She did not hear, because she could not hear, the little click as the lock on the door sprung open. When the light went out, her first reaction was a mumbled "Shit." But then, almost instantly, she knew she was not alone in the pitch-darkness of the windowless bathroom.

"Jamie?" she choked, fumbling for the faucets with fingers that just didn't seem to be working. "Jamie, is that you?" Suddenly a hand was sliding across her belly, into her belly, into her pubic hairs, grabbing. *Oh, my God, oh my God in heaven!* It was squeezing hard in her vulva, hurting.

Blindly, she slapped at the hand once, twice, three times. But it wouldn't let go, and the pain was so great she thought she was going to pass out. With the last of her strength, she got a two-handed grip on the arm, and dug in with her nails, twisting at the same time. There was a little yelp, and she was free, falling, slipping, grabbing madly for whatever might be there to grab. Her left hand found the shower curtain, but couldn't keep it, and she went down hard, hitting the base of her spine, then her head.

Then he was on top of her again, his hands on her breasts, finding the nipples, pinching, and his hard little penis poking into her belly probing clumsily for her vagina. *Oh, no!* Somehow she was still conscious, close to the edge but still aware of the horrible, terrible, unspeakable thing that was happening to her. She got her arms up somehow, and found his throat with an elbow. Then she slipped her knees up under his stomach. With what she knew was the last of her strength, she heaved, and Jamie was flying through the air, crashing down hard on the floor. No, thank God, it was not the last of her strength. She rose and told herself where the door and the light switch were located.

She found the switch and flicked it—just as a powerful hand gripped her right ankle and brought her sliding down the door. But she managed to turn and kick out, and again Jamie went flying. She could see him now, see that once-beautiful face, teeth all bared and blue eyes full of hate and evil. And she wanted to kill him.

For a few seconds they sat there on the floor, breathing in gasps. She was propped up against the door and he was against the opposite wall by the sink. She didn't know if she could fight again. If he got up first, if he came for her, she didn't know if she could stop him this time. Everything hurt so much, her head, her back, her vagina.

Oh please, God, make him stop. Jamie stirred and she braced herself for what she knew would be his final assault. Then, slowly, his expression changed, and she found herself looking into the bewildered face of a little boy again.

"Sandy?" he said hesitantly as if he wasn't sure it really was her, "Sandy, what happened?"

What happened! Oh Jesus Christ! Didn't he know? Did he expect her to believe he didn't know? She couldn't speak. Instead she got to her feet, swayed unsteadily for a few seconds, and then, aware for the first time that she was totally naked, reached for a towel and wrapped it around herself. Jamie stayed where he was blinking uncomprehendingly.

"I love you, Sandy, "he whispered, "I didn't mean to hurt you. I just don't know what happened, honest, Sandy."

"Love me? *Love me?* Are you crazy, Jamie, I..." *My God, he's crazy!*

"Sandy," he was crying now, "what are you going to do? Please don't tell anybody! Please don't tell Barbara and Tom. Please, Sandy, it won't happen again, I know it won't. Please, oh please!"

What should she do? Call the police? Take him to the hospital? What? Tie him up and wait for his parents to come home?

This couldn't happen, none of it. It wasn't possible; it just simply wasn't fucking possible.

"Sandy," he said, his voice a little stronger now, "if you don't tell, I'll do something for you, I promise I will." He crossed his heart. "And hope to die."

"Oh Jamie, Jamie!" What could she do?

"I'll take you to Allan," he said.

"What! You know where Allan is? Where is he? Is he all right?" Suddenly the game had changed and the rules with it. Jamie was pulling himself up, holding onto the sink when she lunged for him, the towel dropping away but she didn't care about that! Clothed or naked, it made no difference. She had Jamie by the throat with both hands and was lifting him off the floor, banging his head against the wall.

"Where is he, you rotten fucking little bastard? Tell me or I'll kill you right now!" Then she relaxed her grip, and her arms fell loosely to her sides. She could not kill this child, no matter what he'd done. A few minutes ago, when she was fighting him for her life, she might have. But not now. "Where, Jamie?" she pleaded softly, "Tell me where."

"I'll have to show you," he said, rubbing absently at his throat. "We'll have to get dressed."

SHE MADE him stay there while she struggled into the jeans and t-shirt she'd been wearing. Then she followed him back into his room and watched his every move while he also put on the same clothes he'd worn earlier in the day. When they left the house, looking for all the world like a big sister and little brother out for a stroll down to McDonald's or Baskin-Robbins or the Colonel's for a treat, the evening sky was going to purple.

"Jamie," she asked as they turned the first corner, "do you really know where Allan is?"

"Yes," he said.

"How do you know?"

"On Saturday, when you were still in bed... Well, he came down to the kitchen and we talked and I told him our secret and—"

"Oh, my God, Jamie, did you take Allan into those woods? " She knew from the newspapers that there *was* a hole, and her mind flashed on Allan, down on the bottom, hurt—maybe hurt really bad—for two, almost three whole days.

"Did he fall, Jamie? Did you push him in?" How could she be asking so calmly, as if they were talking about nothing more important than something that had happened in school that day?

Sandy, no matter what, no matter how bad it is, you have to be calm. You have to get him out, and you have to... "Jamie, is he still alive?"

"Yes, he's okay."

"My God, Jamie, why didn't you tell me, why didn't you tell somebody? What kind of little boy are you?"

"I... I heard you and him doing it that night, Sandy. I was... I was jealous, I guess. I hated him. I wanted to hurt him. Then when I got the chance... I would have told you, honest. I was going to tell you tonight. I went every day. I even brought him some food. It was going to be okay, Sandy, honest it was."

There was no question, the boy was completely and totally insane. Sandy knew in the back of her mind that she should be terrified, she should run away screaming to the nearest house and pound on the door and beg whoever was there to phone the police. But no, not yet. What mattered now was finding Allan.

"Here we are," Jamie said.

She followed him into the forest.

"Hold on to my belt," he said, "I know the way."

Given no other choice, or at least feeling as if she had none, she did as she was told. A couple of minutes later they emerged into the clearing, and stood side by side. In the waning light, she saw a field covered with odd little grass-covered mounds, like bubbles almost.

"Over there," Jamie pointed. She squinted in that direction, but saw nothing more unusual than what she'd already observed in this nasty, funny-smelling place.

With increasing reluctance, she followed the boy and drew alongside him at what appeared to be the largest of the mounds. She could see an opening in the top, and, forgetful of Jamie, she leaned over it, calling Allan's name.

Something thudded against her back, and her call became a scream. She was sliding down the side of the hole, reaching, as she had in the darkened bathroom, for anything that might save her. Her body had shifted and her legs were dangling down into the hole. The long grass came out in her hands, but she grabbed and grabbed and scrambled, driving her fingers madly into the soft earth, only to have it crumble away, then driving in again.

But slowly, inexorably, she was losing ground. Then—oh, thank God—a tree root. One hand on, then the second. She looked up, but all she could see was sky. It was two of three feet to the top, and there was just no way she'd ever make it, unless...

"Jamie, for God's sake! Help me out of here. Don't do this Jamie! Jesus, Jamie, what do you want? I'll do anything you ask."

She saw the head appear, but she couldn't quite make out the expression on his face. Then he spoke, and she knew what that face looked like. She could visualize the exposed teeth and the cold, evil eyes that had stared across at her in the bathroom.

"Anything, Sandy?" the deep, terrible voice asked mockingly. "*Anything*, you say? Well, my sweet young Sandy O'Reilly, maybe you should have thought about that before. Before you fucked your 'good friend' Allan. You want to be with him? Okay. Great."

The root was pulling loose, and Sandy fought frantically for another, better grip, but with a growing, now almost full, understanding that further struggle was pointless.

"Oh My God, I am heartily sorry," she prayed, "for having offended Thee, and I detest my sins most aid sincerely, not only because…" The root broke away and she was falling. "…I have lost all right to Heaven, and deserve the everlasting torments of Hell—"

They were there, waiting. She couldn't see them, but she knew they were there. The hideous, fetid smell came first, then something jagged and sharp touched her face and she just closed her eyes and drifted quickly and gently away.

CHAPTER TWENTY-THREE

JAMIE LEFT the house again just after midnight. He had neatly packed Sandy's clothes and cosmetics and books in the single, soft leather bag she'd arrived with the week before. Not satisfied that the late hour would protect him from observation, especially with the police cars prowling so constantly—the state cops were in town now too, he'd noticed earlier—he stuck to the backyards and hedge breaks and bike paths he knew so well. He left the suitcase, carefully covered over by flattened cardboard boxes and other rubbish, in the big open garbage bin behind the A&P and retraced his steps.

Just a couple more things to do before he could sleep. Abergail's house was still dark. He got the rubber gloves and pulled them on. Then he took the letter from where he'd left it on the kitchen counter and went out again, closing the door silently. He slipped across the street and behind the neighbors' houses until he was once more at Miss Livingstone's place. He could no longer think of it as hers and Abergail's.

He edged along the side of the house, slid over the verandah railing, ducked under the window, just in case, and found the mail slot on the door. He pushed the envelope through, then returned home the way he'd come.

"Well," Teddy greeted him as he entered his own room, "I guess that pretty well wraps it up, eh Jamie?"

"Not quite," Jamie replied. "But we have to get up early in the morning. I've got a couple of things I want to do before school. It's the last day, you know."

AFTER NEARLY AN HOUR of sitting around outside Becker Torrey's closed door, awaiting his turn to be questioned by the three FBI agents who'd arrived in town sometime earlier in the evening, David was fantasizing ways to exhume the body of J. Edgar Hoover and kill him all over again. He could have used that useless hour waiting for the agents—and a dozen more, for that matter—to just begin to catch up on lost sleep. But the phone had jangled him awake shortly after one A.M., and Beck had told him that he was sorry, but David had better get dressed and get back down to the station, 'cause the feds were on the job, all shiny faced and full of their own self-made myths.

Refusal, of course, had been out of the question; but David was able, at least, to stage a minor rebellion, helped along by the fact that all of his uniforms, save the one locked up at the dry cleaners, were lying in smelly heaps around the bedroom. He wore his favorite, ass-patched jeans, a pair of torn sneakers, and the cleanest of his University of Wisconsin T-shirts. And, not to be forgotten, he buckled on his shiny gun belt complete with a big .357 Smith & Wesson, silting butt-forward on his right hip. The FBI guys wouldn't like that, which pleased him. He had showered, mostly so that he could stand his own company, but had refused to shave off his three-day growth of beard.

The muffled voices from Torrey's office, in a company

with his own exhaustion, had just about succeeded in lulling him to sleep in the chair, when all at once a hand was on his shoulder, and he looked up into the grave—more grave than usual—face of Norm Fleischer.

"David," Fleischer half-whispered, "I'd like to talk to you in private for a few minutes. Care to take a short walk?"

Without waiting for an answer he went to the door and opened it, motioning David through. If the night was any cooler than the previous day had been, it wasn't measurable without instruments, and David's lungs had to fight hard to extract what air there was from the heavy humidity. He followed Fleischer down the steps and out into the parking lot, where the sergeant stopped, lit the remains of a fat cigar, and leaned against David's Camaro.

"David," he began, "there's something I think you should know about. It may involve all of the cases we're working on, but, more specifically, it involves a friend of yours. Margaret Livingstone."

Oh Jesus! Margaret's killed herself! And where were you, David Bentley, when she needed you? Sleeping. Sleeping and playing cops and... and what?

"No, David," Fleischer said, reading his mind. "She's not dead; she's in hospital under sedation. But there's a real problem, I have to tell you and I've got to get inside and talk to Beck, so I can't explain it fully. You know that niece of hers, the redhead, Abergail? Well, I think she may be missing person number five."

David stood mute: too many images were spiraling through his head for him to settle on any one of them. So Fleischer continued. "We found Ms. Livingstone walking around the streets in her nightgown about half an hour ago, David. I didn't call that in, because I was afraid you were here and I wanted to tell you personally. She couldn't talk, and I don't think she could really tell who we were, but we had no trouble getting her into the car and to the hospital. The only trouble we had was prying these out of her hand."

David took the crumpled piece of paper first and held it up so that the light from the police station windows made it readable. "*Miss Livingstone*," it said in cutout, "*Abergail is dead. Ha-Ha.*"

David started to crush it angrily in his hand, then stopped and handed it back to Fleischer. Then he took the sad little hank of hair and examined that against the light. Finally, he found some words. "Norm," he said tonelessly, "I've never felt so goddamned helpless—so incapable of doing my job. Jesus."

In a rare show of affection, Fleischer put his hand on David's shoulder and squeezed lightly. Then he walked past him, back up into the station. David sat down heavily on the steps, put his face in his hands, and wept.

JAMIE CLIMBED to his perch for what he knew had to be the last time. He untied the big knot, unwound the rope its seven turns and pulled it free. Then he looped it over the branch he was standing on and played it out until the two ends met, about eight feet from the ground. Hand-over-hand he climbed most of the way down on it, dropped the last few easy feet, and pulled the rope free. He coiled it up, slung it on his shoulder, and walked to the hole.

With his hands he dug away the soft earth that covered most of the tree trunk that had been his vantage point; he tied one end of the rope to a root he figured would never bend or break. Then he played the knotted rope down into the hole.

"Hey, friends," he called and waited, listening. After a few minutes of pig-grunts they were directly below him once again, quiet now, as if waiting for him to open the conversation. Which he did, in his Jamie voice. "I won't be coming here anymore," he said sadly. "We're moving. We're going away. I can't bring you any food..."

"Foord!" came the insistent sound from below. Then a chorus of "foord!"

"No," Jamie said, when the voices had died, "no more food. But I'm setting you free now, to find your own more food..."

"Foord! Foord!"

"Oh yes. There's lots of food up here." He smiled, a little wistfully, and raised his hand in one last wave of good-bye. Then he got up and slowly walked away.

A pair of clawed hands took the rope and pulled.

There was a short, jabbered discussion, with all five participating in their tight little circle. Then, one by one, they began to climb out.

CAREN WOKE FIRST AND, after she'd determined that Greg was still snoring happily beside her, she slid out of the sleeping bag carefully and considerately. She walked a few yards away, loving every barefoot step in the wet morning grass, and faced the red sun that was hanging just above the eastern horizon. She raised her arms to it, went up on her toes, and languorously stretched the stiffness from her naked, unblemished nineteen-year-old body.

What a wonderful world it was, to provide mornings like this one; and *places* like this one. She did a slow turn, taking it all in—the rolling fields to the west and north, interrupted only by remnants of stone walls and split-rail fences, the woods to the south, with its symphony of greens, and the clear, sparkling water of the quarry, surrounded by the red granite walls, already reflecting the light and warmth of the sun.

Buffalo—home—was only three days behind them, as the

motorcycle flies, but it seemed much, much farther away. How lucky they'd been, last night, to turn up this particular old farm road, rather than one of the dozens of others they'd thought about taking. *Maybe,* she thought, *we can stay the whole day. I'd love to see it all at sunset, see if it's as beautiful then as it is now.*

She did one more slow pirouette, surveying her temporary domain as she hoped she would always remember it, then tripped lightly over to the big Honda road bike and fished a bar of soap out of the saddlebag. Before going down to the water's edge, she checked Greg again. He'd shifted a little, and he wasn't snoring, but he was still sleeping soundly.

She dipped in a toe. The water was chilly but warm enough for her. Setting the soap down on the rock, she bent her knees and did a springing dive, cutting the surface cleanly, with only a minimum of splash. Caren was a good swimmer, a strong one who could do a mile at the University of Buffalo pool without even breathing hard. And this, this was better: she felt like she could swim forever and never get tired. About the middle of the quarry pond, thirty yards or so from the where she'd dived in, she rolled over on her back and floated lazily, closing her eyes against the sun and thinking the happiest of thoughts.

When she opened them, Greg was standing on the rock promontory where she'd entered the water, smiling and waving at her. "Hi," she yelled back. "Come on in, it's absolutely gorgeous."

What a beautiful man, she thought, *what a perfect body.* She watched him step down to the water's edge and then, suddenly, from behind him and off to one side, a blur of gray hurled through the air and then Greg was down on the rock, arms and legs thrashing madly; and something hideous and nonhuman was on top of him, screaming sounds that chilled her to the soul and swiping with gnarled, taloned hands.

Instinctively she began swimming toward them, grimly, not crying out, pushing her body beyond its limits.

She didn't see Greg get a hand free and drive it hard into the creature's throat, but when she looked up again, Greg was scrambling to his feet, that beautiful body all torn and bloody, his eyes still wild with shock and fear. She stopped, morbidly fascinated, and treaded water as Greg dropped into the stance that just weeks before had won him his brown belt in karate from the most respected teacher in northern New York. On the large, flat surface of the rock, Greg and the monster circled one another. Greg kicked out twice, so fast that the motion was almost unseeable, but the thing dodged easily and sprang again. Greg stepped left, dropped down, then uncoiled a tremendous backhanded blow that caught the monster in mid-flight, lifted it high in the air, and sent it flying toward… her!

Suddenly a gray, hairy head broke the water in front of Caren, and she was looking into merciless, yellow eyes and a gaping mouthful of rotting, jagged, brown-yellow teeth. Then just as suddenly she was in its grip, being dragged under.

"Greg!" she screamed. "Help me!"

With what was left of her strength, she shoved her right elbow into the thing's throat and, lungs shouting for air, held the ghastly face a few inches back from her own.

Greg, oh Greg, don't let this happen! Greg! Oh my God, this can't be real!

"HAVE A GOOD DAY," the driver said.

"Thanks," Trudy Saywell replied, lifting her backpack onto her shoulder. "You too. And thanks for the ride."

"No problem," he said, slipping the Chevy back into drive and pulling away. "Hope you get another ride soon."

She watched him for a few seconds until the indicator light went on and he turned left toward the town. She sat down cross-legged beside the road and rolled a joint, her first of the day and the first since she'd left Chicago, on the thumb, the night before. She'd have a little smoke, maybe try to loosen her muscles a little from the all-night drive, then get back on the road. Who knows where she'd end up? It didn't matter. She'd go wherever her thumb and friendly drivers took her.

She had just lit the match and was bringing it to the dangling J when a huge dump truck screeched to a halt in front of her, and a man leaped out with a shotgun in his hands.

Oh Christ, she thought, her heart half-exploding, *it's* Easy Rider *all over again!* She threw both match and joint as far as she could and was almost on her feet when the man was in front of her. But he wasn't looking at her, not really; he was looking beyond her, into the woods, squinting. She half turned to look, but she saw nothing. No, wait, there was a little movement there in the bushes. Some kind of animal, a wolf, a bear?

"Did you see that?" the man asked, still not paying that much attention to her beyond the simple acknowledgement that she was there.

"What?" she said, matching his squint now, but unable to see even the movement she thought might have been there just previously.

"Something I've never seen before," he said. "But it was there, I did see it. It was like a man, but a... oh, shit, it looked like a man but it was all covered with gray hair, like some kind of goddamned ape, but it wasn't an ape."

She just stood there, shaking her head uncomprehendingly, and feeling the first pangs of fear that she was in the presence of a madman, a madman with a loaded gun. Should she scream? There were houses nearby; somebody would hear her, surely.

The man grabbed her arm and propelled her toward his truck, and she opened her mouth to cry for help, but his words, which were full of concern, not threat, stopped her.

"Get in," he said, "and lock it up after you. If you see a car, flag it down and tell him to get the cops." Then, even more softly, "Young lady, some terrible things have been going on in this town lately. Terrible things. Now I saw something in there, in Whately's Copse, and I'm going to find out what it is. Now you be smart, you keep yourself safe."

"Who are you?" she asked.

"Nobody. A truck driver. My name's Frank Gorman. Now you get in that truck, and you watch for cars, okay?"

She did as she was told. Two cars went by in a three or four minute period, but despite her frantic waving, neither stopped. Then she heard a gunshot, followed almost instantly by another and, forgetting her orders, she climbed down from the cab and stepped gingerly into the woods, where an old wooden fence had been broken down.

"Mr. Gorman?" she said tentatively. "Mr. Gorman, are you all right?" Pushing away sharp branches with her hands, she moved in a little farther, calling the truck driver's name. To her left she saw something red. Had he been wearing red? No, dark green, both shirt and pants. Nevertheless, she moved toward the red thing, still calling his name, but even more hesitantly than before.

"Mr. Gorman! Oh no, oh no!" His throat had been torn away and his face was awash with blood. His chest was still rising and falling, but irregularly, and it was making a rattling, gurgling sound. Trudy opened her mouth to scream, but that was as far as it got.

Unseen, from above, the creature pounced, sinking its long, jagged teeth into her neck, and driving her face down onto the ground. The terrible thing, she thought, before the oblivion mercifully came, the really terrible thing was that she could feel herself being eaten. And hear it.

DAVID HAD JUST LEFT the hospital, and his mind was full of Margaret, How incredibly sad she had looked, lying Where all doped up, just staring and unable to speak sobbing silently sometimes. What would happen? he'd asked the young psychiatrist. We just don't know for sure, the doctor had said. He had tried to be reassuring, and David had tried to appreciate it, but…

"Christ, that sounded like gunshots," He tramped the accelerator of the hill, just before Whately's Copse, to see a big gravel truck half in the ditch and what looked like a young girl entering the woods. He jumped on the brake pedal, sending the Camaro into a four-wheel lock and the fastest stop possible, and the tires were still screeching when he had the radio microphone in his hands, demanding as many men as possible at Whately's Copse. He didn't even wait for an acknowledgement; he was around the car, opening the trunk, and snatching the five-shot, 12-gauge from its spring brackets on the lid.

He pumped a shell into the chamber as he plunged into the woods, calling after the girl. He was getting cut up pretty badly, but he paid no attention to the blood or the pain; that would come later, if at all. Something he saw, something he heard, made him swing to the left and suddenly he was looking into the yellow eyes of his waking nightmare, and at a mouth still chewing a bloody chunk of human flesh. He fired from the hip and the creature flew backward through the air, landing in a heap, half of its chest blown away. Then, incredibly, it rose to its feet and started toward him again. He lifted the shotgun to his shoulder and aimed carefully. This time he blew its head off, and this time it did not get up.

Then he saw the man and the girl. The man—he thought it was Frank Gorman, but he couldn't tell because of all the blood—was dead. The girl, the one he'd seen enter the woods, was still breathing, but there was a huge deep wound on the back of her neck, the blood spurting rhythmically from an unseen severed artery. David dropped the shotgun and knelt beside her, feeling for the artery, trying to staunch the flow before she bled to death, as she almost certainly would in a very short time.

David caught the movement to his right, but it was too late to do anything about it other than raise an arm. The jagged teeth caught it, and he could feel them break down, down, through flesh and muscle all the way to the bone. Clawed hands grasped for his face, ripping away skin, and clawed feet kicked at him, shredding cloth, driving in, holding on like some fear-crazed cat.

David, shoving the horror away from him as best he could, knowing his only hope—small as it was—lay in keeping the creature on his forearm, reached across his body with the left hand, found the magnum, cocked it and pressed the muzzle right between the yellow eyes. He squeezed the trigger.

The lifeless creature still dangled from his arm. The hole in its forehead was no bigger than a third of an inch or so in diameter. The back of its head, however, was gone. Using the gun barrel as a lever, he pried the dead jaws open, and fighting against a pain that nearly made him faint, pulled the jagged teeth out of his arm. Blood—but fortunately not much of it, meaning major veins and arteries had been spared—flowed down over his hand. The arm, from the elbow down, was numb and almost, but not quite, useless.

Somewhere behind him a lot of car doors were slamming, and his name was being shouted over an electric bullhorn. He recognized Beck Torrey's voice, and he shouted back. Somehow, David gathered the girl into his arms—arm, actually, with the right just doing what it could—and staggered blindly through the woods toward the voices. Then somebody was taking the girl from him, and somebody else was holding him up, leading him out. The world started to swim and go very dark, then it stabilized itself and he was face-to-face with Beck Torrey.

"Monsters," David gasped, trying to forget even more than he was trying to remember. "Whately's. The hole. Oh, Jesus Christ, Beck. Oh Jesus Christ!"

"Come on, David, come on and sit down. The ambulance is on the way. You're going to be okay. Now take it easy."

But the girl, what about the girl? He tried to get past Torrey, to where he could see her lying on the ground. Helen was bent over her. Helen looked up at him, and shook her head.

Then, finally, the world went away. Beck Torrey Caught the slumping body and lowered it to the ground.

"Somebody get a blanket," he shouted, "and where in the Christ is that goddamned ambulance?"

Rifles, shotguns, and handguns were exploding all over the woods as David was lifted onto the stretcher and whisked rapidly away.

"Kill them. Beck," he mumbled through his semi consciousness. "Kill the fuckers. Kill them, Beck, promise me you'll kill them all!"

"We will, Dave," Torrey said, "we will."

TOM AND BARBARA burst through the door almost side by side, shouting for their son. And there he was, sitting at the kitchen table, drinking a glass of milk, looking somewhat surprised by their strange entrance, but far from wide-eyed with astonishment.

"Oh, thank God, Jamie!" Barbara said, skidding to a halt on the yesterday-polished floor. "Thank God you're all right!'

"Sure," he said, matter-of-factly, "I'm fine. What's the matter?"

"Oh, Jamie, all the terrible things. We saw a newspaper at the airport. We drove ninety miles an hour all the way home, listening on the radio. Oh, Jamie, how awful it must have been for you, your school friends disappearing. And Miss Oliphant, and—"

"They weren't my friends," Jamie said, taking another sip of his milk.

Then, for the first time, Tom spoke. "Where's Sandy?" he asked, looking around the room as if she might be hiding up in the cupboards or behind the refrigerator.

"She left this morning," Jamie replied. "With her boyfriend. His name is Allan."

"She left you with all this going on?" Barbara simply could not believe that anybody, especially somebody like Sandy, who'd seemed so bright and responsible and capable, would walk out on a twelve-year-old boy. Even Jamie? Even Jamie. "What kind of monster is she, anyway?"

"Oh no, mom, she isn't a monster. We had a good time together. It was great, really great. Honest."

Barbara and Tom exchanged glances. He nodded, and she turned back to Jamie, who was on the way to the sink to wash her glass.

"Jamie," she said, "your father and I talked it over in the car, and we decided that you and I should leave for Seattle now, today. Is that all right with you?"

"Sure," he said, almost indifferently, more interested in drying the glass—or so it seemed—than this wonderful idea of his mother's. "But first I better go down and clean out my terrarium, and let the toads and snakes go. It wouldn't be fair to keep them there if I'm not around to feed them."

THE FIRST THING David saw when he came to was the last thing he saw before he collapsed—Becker Torrey's unsmiling face.

"Can you move your fingers?" Torrey asked, which was a bit strange, David thought, for an opener, especially under the circumstances. He tried and he could.

"That's good," Torrey said. "I'll tell the doctors."

Doctors? Oh, yeah, he was in hospital. It was all white and clean. He was fully conscious now and working at some important questions.

"How bad was it, Beck?"

"Two dead—Frank Gorman and the girl you tried to save —and three wounded, including you."

"Three?"

"Yeah. A couple of kids from Buffalo camped overnight by the quarry. They were swimming this morning when one of those things attacked them. The boy killed it with his bare hands, in the water, just as it was dragging the girl under. They arrived on their motorcycle just a few minutes after you were taken away. A bit cut up, but not as bad as you. They'll need the shots too."

"Shots? What shots? Tetanus?"

"Rabies, Dave. Those things might have been rabid."

David knew damn right well that if the creatures had been rabid, a quick and simple test of their bodies would establish it. "What do you mean, 'might have been'? Either they were rabid or they weren't."

Torrey drew a long breath, and let it roll back out. "David, remember what I told you about my great grandmother, about things that I couldn't understand but that I had to accept?"

"Come on, Beck, out with it. What are you trying to say, anyway?"

"They're gone, David. Not a sign of them, just a few pieces of tissue and some blood we were able to collect on leaves and bark and that sort of thing. I didn't see it, but Pedersen and Cogan did, and you can believe it if you want to: just as they broke into the clearing they saw two live ones carrying the dead ones down into that hole. By the time they got there, the things were gone. They—Pedersen and Cogan and half a dozen other guys—just emptied their guns into the place. Then Cogan went down. There was a rope there, David, a knotted rope. Somebody let them up!"

David fell back onto the pillow and threw his good arm across his eyes. No, of course this couldn't be real, nothing in the past five days could have been real. I'll just close my eyes and when I open them, Beck'll be gone and I'll be at home in bed, waking up with a hangover.

Torrey was still there.

Oh shit!

Torrey was holding out a pair of dark glasses. He turned them slightly in his hand so that David could see the name taped to the armature: Miss Emma Oliphant. "Cogan found these," he said, "half-buried down there."

"Anything else?" David swallowed.

"No, nothing. He saw three tunnels, but he wouldn't go in, even if he could have."

"So where do we go from here?"

"It's already underway, Dave. I've got machinery going in there now. We'll have to dig up the whole field, probably."

"And sow the ground with salt," David whispered.

"What was that?"

"Nothing." Torrey was getting up to go when David remembered his very last question.

"Beck, you said you got some blood samples. Can they tell yet what kind of animal those things were?"

Torrey stopped and turned slowly. He looked David in the eye and said in a still-disbelieving voice. "The tests so far

have been only preliminary, but it appears the blood is
human."

CHAPTER TWENTY-FOUR

Jamie woke just before sunrise, and it took him a few minutes to figure out just where he was. Oh yeah, Seattle, on the farm, their new home. They'd arrived last night, him and Barbara—and Teddy, of course—and Tom was coming along as soon as he could. Jamie slipped out of bed and went to the window; the first muted rays of sunlight were spreading out on the eastern horizon.

"Morning, Jamie," Teddy said behind him.

"Hi, Teddy. What do you think of this place?"

"Not bad, partner, not bad at all."

"Hey." Jamie smiled, "how about we go out and explore, before Barbara gets up. It should be great here, Teddy, for us, I mean. Nobody else around. You can come with me lots of times, not like back home… er, not like back in Wisconsin."

"Yes," Teddy said, "let's do that."

He dressed and gathered the bear into his arms, stopped in the hallway to get his bearings, then slipped quietly downstairs. They were halfway across the yard, heading toward the barn, when an unfamiliar voice behind them said, "Hello, you must be Jamie."

Standing there was probably the most beautiful little girl

he had ever seen, all dressed in pure white, so beautiful that she made his throat go dry and his stomach set a warm watery. And the strange thing was she was just a kid, like him. Younger even, maybe only ten. Who was she? Where had she come from? What was she doing there, on his farm, at five or six o'clock in the morning?

She moved closer, and with every step she grew more and more lovely. There seemed to be a soft mist around her, and her feet hardly seemed to touch the ground.

"Uh… yes," he stammered, "I'm… uh… Jamie. And this is… uh… Teddy. He's my friend."

"My name is Alicia," she said. Her voice was like a little bell, a bell made of crystal and gold. "I live down the road, and I often go out for early walks. I love the morning, especially before the sun comes up."

"Uh, me too," he said, feeling foolish and not quite sure whether or not he did love the early morning, because it was the first time he'd ever thought about it.

"I know a secret," she said, cocking her perfect blond head to one side. "Do you want to see it?"

"Sure," Jamie said, suddenly more sure of himself. "I know some secrets too. We'll share."

"Okay," she said, "but first you have to cross your heart and hope to die."

Oh, he thought, doing so, *this is all going to be just great!*

She led him and Teddy across the fields and into a woods about a quarter-mile from where his mother lay sleeping. On the other side was a creek, and beside the creek, a very familiar-looking mound of earth. Alicia waved him closer, and they stood together on the lip, looking down into an equally familiar black hole.

"There are creatures down there," she said very seriously, brushing her hand against his and sending happy little electric waves through his body.

"I know!" he said, doubly excited. "They're trogs—troglodytes!"

"Yes," she said, her mouth close to his ear, "that's just what they are." Then she stepped back and gave him a little push. Just enough. Then he was gone.

She gathered Teddy into her arms and walked slowly away. She stopped at the bank of the creek, pulled off her shoes and stockings and dangled her tiny feet in the cool water.

"Well, Teddy," she said, "unless you have other plans, you can come home with me."

"That'll be fine," Teddy replied.

"My, what a nice voice you have. You sound just like an actress. I wish I had a voice like that."

"You will," Teddy said. "You will."

9 781966 037552